Trace & Tori

THE SHADOWDANCE CLUB 4

AVERY GALE®

DEDICATION

For my husband... who knows first-hand the source of stories of Tori's disastrous cooking escapades.

You have no doubt earned a special "dining spot" in heaven!

Chapter 1

Trace Bartell was one of the few Doms at The ShadowDance Club everybody liked and respected. Club owners, Alex and Zach Lamont had always maintained anyone who thought ranchers weren't multitalented, versatile businessmen, capable of stepping into almost any situation and making it fly had never met the man known locally as *The Gentle Giant*. Bartell was known for always being cool under pressure, and his aptitude for business was widely regarded as nothing short of brilliant.

After losing his wife, going on three years ago, when she'd been run off the road by a drunken teenager from a neighboring community, the man had done the unthinkable and become the young offender's advocate. Even though he had been devastated by his loss, he had lobbied the prosecutor and judge to impose a sentence requiring the young man to work on his ranch for nothing but room and board for a year and perform a thousand hours of community service.

Trace talked to numerous members of the teen's community and discovered the kid had been considered a problem in his hometown for years. Everybody he'd talked to said they'd expected the young man to fail, and damn if the kid hadn't tried his hardest to prove all the naysayers right.

Miraculously, the year he spent on the Bartell Ranch had turned the kid around. Trace taught him values and was even helping fund his college education. When people had asked him why he'd done it, he assured everyone it had been healing for them both. Trace reasoned imprisoning the kid would have changed the tragic accident that stole his loving wife into a double fatality.

Everyone who knew him hoped Trace would find a woman who would appreciate the kind spirit still mourning the loss of a great love. Trace Bartell's kindness and generosity earned the respect of everyone he came in contact with.

Trying for years to buy the small ranch next to his had proved to be an exercise in futility when the elderly owner consistently, but always politely refused even his most generous offers. The house had been little more than a shack before it burned to the ground recently, but Saul Paulson had been steadfast in his insistence someday his family was going to need the place. He'd often referred to his modest acreage as the "thing that will be that young gal's saving grace."

Trace never understood the man's ramblings even though they'd been neighbors as long as Trace could remember, and he'd never known any family members to visit the elderly rancher. While Trace's parents had lived on the ranch, his mother always invited their neighbors for holidays.

Smiling to himself, Trace remembered the celebrations his family had shared with their neighbors and friends. Their home had been a virtual cornucopia of anyone in or around their hometown who didn't have a family of their own to celebrate with. Some of his fondest childhood memories were based in those mixed-up holiday observations.

When Saul passed away a few months ago, Trace had made inquiries again and been told the old man had left his entire estate to a family member living in Texas. He'd been told Victor Paulson was a Harvard-educated attorney who was expected in town later today. Trace had wondered briefly what had happened to the woman the old guy had so often referred to but had come to the conclusion it was useless to think about the wanderings of another man's mind.

TRACE COULD HONESTLY say he couldn't remember the last time he'd been completely blindsided by anything other than his wife's death. But damn if it hadn't happened today. Finding out Victor Paulson was, in fact, Victoria Paulson, the beautiful woman he'd found sitting in front of the local tavern had been the best news he'd had since he lost his sweet Nan.

The electricity that raced up his arm when he'd helped her up off the snowy bench shocked him. He was convinced Tori had felt it too when he'd heard her soft gasp. Trace had recognized the instant connection he felt with Tori, and his only explanation was his friends' predictions Nan would send him an angel had finally come true.

The hour he'd spent away from her while he'd helped with the craziness of the local Dominatrix trying to shoot one of The ShadowDance Club's subs had been excruciating. He'd known from the first moment he saw Tori sitting out in the snow looking like she'd lost her best friend, their mutual attraction was too strong to ignore.

Discovering everything she owned in the world was in that piece of shit car she'd been driving created more questions than it answered. *Why in the hell is a Harvard-educated lawyer basically living out of her car?* It just didn't make any sense, and he made a mental note to contact Mitch Grayson at ShadowDance to see what he could find out.

Mitch was a friend and fellow Dom; furthermore, he would be discreet. Trace had heard The Club's owners laugh about how their resident communications and computer guru had access to information legitimate law enforcement agencies could only dream about.

Sitting in Trace Bartell's Dodge pickup, staring out into the inky darkness, Tori wondered if she'd lost her ever-loving mind. After the toe-curling drive through the mountains over highways that should really be labeled as roller coaster paths for cars, she'd found herself homeless in a matter of minutes after arriving in the picturesque small town named Climax, of all things. Then she'd agreed to go home with a complete stranger… and that had to be one of the most impulsive decisions she'd ever made in her entire life. But there was something about the man she was drawn to, it was as if they were kindred spirits. She sensed a sadness in him, a remoteness that was hauntingly familiar.

Thinking back to the moment when she'd seen the sign on the office door of the town's only attorney wishing her a "Happy Thanksgiving" and saying he'd meet her the next Wednesday, she'd almost burst into tears. She had known without the elderly attorney's key to the home she had recently inherited, she was going to have to find another place to stay for a few days and was already running on fumes. With exhaustion threatening to overtake her, she'd made her way into the nearby tavern. When she'd been told the house she planned to live in had burned down, Tori's world came crashing down around her.

She'd dealt with losing her mother to cancer, her father's death because of his own stupidity, and a year of hell at the hands of a stalker. Still, she could count on one hand the number of times she'd wanted to just give up, sit down, and sob. Learning she was homeless in a strange town during what was rapidly becoming a blizzard was just too much.

Sitting on the cold bench in front of the small bar, Tori had felt the weight of the world pressing in on her. Trace had stepped out of the shadows, his calm questions and deep voice pulling her back from the edge of despair. She hadn't had anyone to rely on since her mom died when she was only fifteen, and she'd been surprised at how good it had felt when Trace had wrapped her in his arms. He'd simply held her when he'd seen her tears earlier in the small diner where he'd taken her, so she could warm up and he could feed her.

In the back of her mind, she'd known it was dangerous to trust a man she didn't know. Hell, that's how she'd ended up with the stalker from hell, but she could sense a strong and honorable spirit surrounding this man, and it spoke directly to her soul. Sighing, she realized she had two choices at this point, trust the man she was riding with or jump out of the truck into the freezing cold. *Cripes, I must be more exhausted than I thought if I see jumping out of a moving vehicle as an option.*

Tori found herself drifting closer and closer to total

relaxation. The warmth of the truck cab, the clean, masculine scent of the gorgeous man sitting next to her, and her full stomach were letting her slowly sink into oblivion. Deciding that she'd sort through all her problems later, Tori let her eyes drift shut and finally surrendered herself to the exhausted sleep her body was craving.

Chapter 2

Trace knew immediately when Tori finally fell asleep by the way her breathing had leveled out. He'd been able to almost feel the tension radiating off her and had been grateful when sheer exhaustion finally claimed her. Driving up the long, tree-lined drive leading to the ranch, he marveled at the almost mystical beauty of the landscape surrounding him.

Chuckling to himself when he realized this was the same view he saw every day, he marveled at how much more beautiful it seemed when he thought about seeing it through Tori's eyes. Having her sleeping peacefully beside him opened up a whole new world of possibilities. He'd almost given up finding a woman who made him *feel* again. After all, what were the chances of finding another woman to love with the passion and depth that he'd enjoyed with Nan? Could lightning strike twice in the same man's heart?

Sighing as he pulled up in front of his log and stone-covered ranch home, he took just a minute to look at the beautiful residence he and Nan had just started building when he'd lost her. Finishing it had been pure torture, hell, there'd been moments he'd wanted to bulldoze the entire thing off the side of the mountain. But now, knowing he was going to be sharing it, even if only platonically with Tori, somehow, made all those agonizing months of construction seem worthwhile.

Shaking his head at his odd musings, he quietly exited the truck and moved around to the passenger side. Reaching in and releasing her safety belt, he looked at her sweet face. Her features were softened in sleep, and she looked exactly like the angel he'd first thought her to be. The wariness was gone, and she was so beautiful, she stole his breath. Her skin was almost luminous in the muted lights coming from the large, wrap-around front porch of his home. The warm amber of the lights danced around them, giving everything a sense of warmth despite the frigid temperature. The snow was falling heavily, and the view in front of him looked like something out of a Norman Rockwell painting.

Sliding his arms under her, Trace picked Tori up into his arms and was overwhelmed at how right she felt cuddled against his chest as he carried her inside. Laying her gently on the soft leather sofa facing the fireplace, he covered her with the worn quilt he kept nearby. The quilt had been a gift from his maternal grandmother and it had been one of his most treasured possessions since he'd been a young boy. He tucked the soft, well-worn fabric around Tori and let her sleep while he carried her meager possessions to the guest suite. After he put his truck in the garage and secured the house for the night, Trace sat on the low table facing the sofa for long moments, watching the little snow princess sleep.

The fire in the stone hearth sent flickering light dancing over the dark waves of her hair, making the red highlights come alive. Her cheeks were finally showing a healthy glow as the flames warmed them. He could see deep purple circles shadowing under her eyes, so prominent, they looked like bruises, making him wonder when she'd last had a good night's sleep.

Promising to make sure she got plenty of rest and plenty of healthy food, he made a mental note to remind her of the importance of taking good care of herself. He sighed and finally gave into temptation and drew his fingers down the side of her face in a light caress, enjoying her small shiver before she leaned closer, seeking his touch. *See, princess, your body already knows you are safe with me, now we just need to get your head and heart on board.*

Trace carefully scooped her back up into his arms and held her tightly against his chest as he made his way to the guest suite's lavish bath. There was something about carrying a sub Trace had always felt conveyed a powerful message. In his mind, the small act had a strong dual meaning—it spoke clearly about who was in control, and it ensured a sub felt cherished. Trace knew it was imperative a sub felt safe giving over her control to her Dom. The lifestyle was all about trust.

When he set Tori on the counter, he leaned her back against the gigantic mirror and had her shoes and socks off by the time her eyelids started to flutter open.

"Welcome back, *again*, sweetheart. I thought you might like to take a quick shower, then you can get ready for bed. I'll get you something to wear and be right back."

"Wait! You're going to come back in here? While I'm in the shower?" Her voice sounded like she was frightened, but the arousal in her eyes was broadcasting an entirely different message. "I mean, I know it's your house and everything, but... well, I'm not really that... well, I mean... I know I'm..."

Trace was sure he had to be wrong. This gorgeous woman couldn't possibly be ashamed of the way she looked, could she? He could have understood if she'd felt unsure of having a strange man in the room for safety reasons, but this? Stepping forward again so that he stood directly in front of her, he placed his hands on both sides of her face.

"Darlin', please tell me someone hasn't made you feel like you are anything but a very beautiful, desirable woman. You are perfect, and if anyone has told you differently, please don't listen to their foolishness."

Tearing down others had long been one of Trace's biggest pet peeves. Why people felt the need to hurt others with words had always been a mystery to him. He'd always believed in the old adage you reap what you sow, so he'd always tried to sow seeds of kindness. When Tori continued to stare at her hands, he moved his fingers beneath her chin and lifted her face to his.

"Princess, you are so beautiful, I keep wondering if you are real. Now please, get your sweet self undressed and into that shower before I do it for you. I'll be back in just a couple of minutes. Don't worry about a towel because I'll be bringing you a warm one from my bathroom down the hall when I return." He heard her soft intake of breath as he walked from the room and knew he might have surprised her, but the fact she wasn't cursing and running from the room told him she was either interested or too stunned to react.

When Trace returned less than five minutes later, he stood just inside the bathroom, watching her silhouette through the shower's lightly frosted door. Victoria Paulson wasn't tall or rail thin, she had beautiful, full breasts that would fit perfectly in his large hands, and her narrow waist tapered to lush hips that appeared absolutely perfect for cradling a man as he stroked deep into her sweet depths.

Her ass was softly rounded with just enough padding

to be perfect for a little paddling play when the mood struck them. His wayward cock responded immediately when he pictured his hand turning her ass cheeks a nice, warm shade of pink. He'd lay her over his lap because that was such a vulnerable and personal position for a woman, then he'd have her part her legs, so he could trace her swollen folds and tease her between swats. By the time he'd finished her erotic spanking, she'd be so close to orgasm, he would only need to give her permission before she'd fly apart in his arms.

When he noticed she'd been leaning against the wall for a few minutes without moving, he opened the shower door and reached in, turning off the water. When she realized the water had stopped, Tori slowly raised her face from where it had been resting on her folded arms and turned her unfocused gaze to face him. *Jesus, Joseph, and Mary—she is a damned vision. How can she not know how desirable she is?*

"Come here, princess... let's get you wrapped in this warm towel. I'll help you dry off, then comb out your beautiful hair while you sit on the bed, how's that sound?"

Trace dried her with gentle pats, then led her into the adjoining bedroom and settled her between his legs on the bed as he combed through her beautiful long hair until it was laying in long strands down her back. He had always loved combing through Nan's hair. Savoring the chance to have a sweet woman nestled between his legs was always a pleasure in his opinion.

Trace had brought Tori one of his shirts, mostly because he'd simply wanted to see her in something of his. He could have rifled through her suitcases to find a gown, but there was something very sensual about seeing a woman in a man's shirt he'd always found extremely sexy.

Nan had always wanted to wear his shirts to bed on the rare occasions he'd allowed her to wear anything at all, and he found he longed to see the soft fabric caressing Tori's tight nipples, the soft swell of her belly, and the dark curls above her sex showing through the shirt that had been thinned to the point it was almost sheer from frequent washings. As he slid the towel from around her and placed the soft T-shirt over her head, he watched her nipples tighten to sharp points and saw her breathing hitch.

As he stepped back and started to turn to leave, she whispered, "Thank you." Her voice sounded soft, and he had the feeling there was more she wanted to say but was hesitant. She finally added, "I'm so grateful to you for all you've done... and well... I..." He waited patiently because even though Tori seemed about to give up finishing her sentence, there was a note of hesitance again. She finally sighed deeply and reached out for him.

"Could I have another hug, please? I've had, well, it's been a kind of rough few months and well, your hugs are really... um, comforting and I am... well, I just..." Trace saw the tears start to fill her pretty eyes and reached up to caress his fingers over her flushed cheeks. "I'm sorry. I'm tired, and I cry when I'm tired, and I..." she didn't get to finish before he'd pulled her into his arms.

Trace savored the feel of Tori's softness as he wrapped her in his embrace. She smelled of citrus, sage, and sweet woman, and he let her scent fill his senses. He savored those long minutes before he spoke.

"Sweetness, I want you to promise me you will never apologize again for needing a hug from me. You are a beautiful woman, and I love holding you, and the fact it's comforting for *both* of us is just icing on the cake." He smiled down at her and was pleased to see the relief in her expression while he gently moved her back toward the large bed. He pulled back the covers and settled her in before covering her, tucking the covers in around her. When Trace started to move away from her, Tori grabbed his hand and looked deep into his eyes.

"Please, stay with me for a while. I'm not usually so needy, I swear, but I just don't want to fall asleep alone. And when you go, please leave a light on. I've gotten used to sleeping with a light, so I could get to my emergen... um... well, I just need to be able to see where things are... it helps me sleep."

Tori hadn't meant to mention the months she'd spent too terrified to close her eyes and give into restful sleep. The man who had stalked her had turned her life upside-down, and she wasn't sure she would ever be the same again. All those nights of lying awake, wondering if this would be the night he finally came into her home and did all the vile things he'd promised he would do to her had taken a huge toll. At one point, Tori had been so exhausted, she'd fallen into such a deep sleep sitting in her car at a traffic light. She hadn't realized people were gathered around her car, thinking she'd died. When the policeman they'd called finally roused her, they'd insisted she be taken by ambulance to the nearest hospital, so she could be screened for medical issues that might cause her to be a hazard to others while driving. The whole thing had been so humiliating, Tori had nearly packed up and moved that very afternoon.

The play of emotions over Tori's face squeezed his heart, making him wonder who the prick was who'd make this lovely woman afraid of her own shadow. Someone had tried to convince her she was less than desirable, so she'd be humbled and grateful for his attention, and when that hadn't worked, he'd terrorized her. He didn't know who, but he'd seen it with submissives too many times now not to recognize the signs in Victoria Paulson. Abusive men were in abundance everywhere but here in Climax.

The small town he called home made short work of any man who thought to abuse a woman or a child with physical or emotional cruelty. Trace had seen examples of both types of abuse and was convinced the scars caused by emotional battering were far worse because that type of abuse was so easy to hide, it could, and often did, go undetected for years.

Emotional batterers whittled away the very essence of their victim until those on the receiving end often couldn't even recall what their own likes and dislikes had once been. Essentially, their true identities had been systematically erased by the person abusing them. He'd listened as Alex and Zach's mother, Catherine Lamont recalled the stories of women she worked with at the shelter in Denver the Lamont family funded. Those stories never failed to remind Trace of the importance of the rigid screening and training requirements that were strictly enforced at The ShadowDance Club.

A submissive's natural desire to please others could easily be misinterpreted by a Dominant who didn't value the gift he'd been given. The sub's vulnerability was a siren's call to both honorable sexual Dominants and assholes alike—their motives and goals the only difference. Doms wanted to enhance a sub's sexual pleasure and enrich her life while abusers were focused on controlling every aspect of their victim's life.

Trace often coached subs on how to tell the difference between a true Dom and a wannabe who was, usually, nothing more than an abusive asshole. At that moment,

Trace was hit full force with a need to protect Tori so strong, it shocked him. He'd already set his contacts to work checking her out, and he was willing to bet there was going to be at least one abuser not too far behind all her fears.

"Darlin', I can only think of a couple of things I'd like better than to hold you while you fall asleep, but I'm not going to mention those just yet." His smile was meant to let her know she was safe with him, and it appeared to have worked because her expression was sleep-soft and just a little loopy.

He lay alongside her and pulled her close, so her head rested on his shoulder, his arm wrapped around her shoulder to hold her tightly against his side. He felt her relax and knew she was drifting off. Knowing she'd trusted him enough to surrender herself to sleep while he held her warmed him to his soul.

"Sleep, my sweet snow angel. You'll always be safe with me." Tori must have heard his softly whispered words through the fog of sleep because he saw a hint of a smile when he pressed his soft lips against her forehead.

Trace didn't want to leave her, he loved the feel of her cuddled against him, but he needed to make a few calls and get cleaned up. He would check on her again before returning to his own room. Shifting away from her, he'd stroked the hair back from her face until she was settled and sleeping once again.

Before leaving the room, he dimmed the lights so there was just enough light, she'd know where she was in case she woke up frightened. He had just finished his shower after reminding his foreman he was covering for him tomorrow when he heard a bloodcurdling scream that had him running to Tori's room like the hounds of hell were hot on his tail.

Throwing open the door, he realized he had only heightened her fear when he'd crashed into the room. Seeing her cowering in the corner, trying to make herself invisible brought him to an abrupt halt. When he slowly moved toward her, she covered her head with her hands and begged him not to shoot her. *What the fuck happened to you baby? Whatever it was, I'll fix it, I promise you.* Startled by his own thoughts, he moved to squat in front of her and pulled her arms gently open, so he could see her tear-stained face. The look of abject terror on her face would haunt him forever.

"Shhh, Tori. It's me, Trace. Princess, I need you to wake up, right now." He'd tried lacing the last sentence with a bit of his Dom voice, hoping she'd respond, and she did exactly as he'd expected. Recognition seemed to wash over her, and she launched herself into his waiting arms. Trace had been sure she was a natural submissive, and her immediate response was all the proof he needed. "That's it, sweetheart. Let me hold you, you had a bad dream, and your scream took several years off my life. I need to hold you for a few minutes and see if I can get my heart rate back somewhere close to normal."

Like every true sub he'd ever known, she was immediately compliant when it meant doing something to help her Dom. Subs were by nature giving and would typically go to great extremes—often at huge personal costs—to keep those around them happy and to be helpful. They almost always went well above and beyond in their attempts to pacify anyone who was unhappy with them and valued harmony above anything self-serving. He'd talked with many Doms over the years who claimed they spent a lot of time protecting their subs from others who would have taken advantage of the submissive's accommodating nature.

When she finally calmed, he picked her up in his arms and moved toward his bedroom. He felt her stiffen slightly, so he hugged her tightly.

"I want you in my bed, Tori. You'll sleep better in my arms, and I know I'll sleep better knowing you are safe. I promise you, nothing is going to happen you don't want to happen, all right?" When she finally nodded her agreement, he continued, "Ordinarily, I'd make you speak the words aloud, but I think we both need a minute to get back on an even keel, so that nod is going to work just fine tonight."

As he turned into the master suite, he saw her eyes take in her surroundings as if she was figuring out all the exits and escape routes as he set her on the edge of the bed. Knowing she wouldn't sleep until she understood the lay of the land, he pointed out the closed door that led to the bathroom and indicated the door they'd just come through.

"Those curtains cover patio doors that lead to a deck overlooking the back of the house, and there is a hot tub out there as well. But right now, I want to lie next to you and hold you in my arms, so we can both get some sleep."

He left his boxer shorts on, but as he pulled her against his bare chest, he slid his hands under the soft cotton shirt, so they spanned her bare back. Her skin felt like warm silk against his fingers, taking in the feel of each beat of her heart and every breath she took.

"God, you feel so good in my arms. You are so beautiful, you simply take my breath away. Just let me hold you while we get some rest, princess. You are and will always be safe with me." He'd no sooner spoken the words, he felt her lips press a small kiss to his bare chest.

"Oh, damn. Tori, please don't start something you don't want me to act on because I'm telling you now, my control is hanging by a thread." Trace was sure Tori felt his cock harden even more against her as he'd spoken his words of caution. She was pushing him, and it had been so long since he'd wanted to make sweet love to a woman, Trace wasn't sure he was going to be able to resist her.

"It's had been so long since I have felt safe in a man's arms, and you make me feel desirable, and I want to lose myself in that intimacy and connection, even if it's only for a little while. Please? I need you…" She'd spoken the words so softly at first, he wasn't sure he'd heard her right, but then he knew he had when she tilted her face up and licked her lips in anticipation.

Chapter 3

T RACE SLOWLY ROLLED Tori beneath him and covered her mouth with his. He kept his kiss tender, but when he felt her soft moan vibrate against his chest, he deepened the kiss with a fervor he knew conveyed his possessive side. Tori's lips were soft, sweet, and plump against his, their warmth making visions of what they would look like wrapped around his cock flash in his mind. Images of her looking up at him as he pushed himself deep into the hot cavern of her mouth made his cock ache to make it a reality. Seeing her dark eyes unfocused with arousal as he held her still while he stroked to the back of her sweet mouth until he could feel her open her throat in surrender flashed through his mind at the speed of light.

Before he let himself get sucked into that fantasy, he moved his mouth to her temple before trailing sweet kisses down the curve her jawline to the other side where he continued kissing down the side of her neck. Reaching that sensitive spot where her neck and shoulder met, he bit gently, then immediately soothed the spot with his tongue.

"Princess, tell me what you need. I'll give you that and so much more, but I need to hear your words." His kept his voice gentle because he was sure she was quickly getting lost in the sensations, so if he was going to get any help from her, he knew he had better get it quickly.

"Oh please… I need… I just need you to…" Tori was already too lost in the sensations swamping her, and it gave him a certain satisfaction knowing she couldn't even think straight enough to form a coherent sentence.

How does he expect me to think when his mouth is painting passion over my skin like he is some kind of Renaissance master or something? Oh my God! At first, I thought maybe I'd just forgotten what it felt like, but I've never felt a connection like this before, and its power swamps me.

"Tori, look at me." When her eyes didn't open, he pulled back from her. "Victoria, you need to open your eyes, so I know you are listening. It's important for many reasons that I will explain later, but right now, I need to know you really want this. Tell me what it is that you need." Trace was well known at the ShadowDance Club as a gentle Dom who was always able to take his subs where they needed to go, but his approach was unlike any of the other Dominants at The Club. He rarely punished a sub with implements or heavy-handed pain, preferring to use positive reinforcements or touch deprivation to get the behaviors he valued.

Slowly, Tori seemed to regain focus, and when she opened her beautiful eyes, Trace was struck by the stark loneliness he saw reflected in their depths. He realized, in that instant, this was a woman who had seen her whole world taken apart, and he knew, instinctively, she needed this connection in a way only another lost soul could truly understand.

"I need you to make love to me, to help me feel desirable again. I need to lose myself in your arms even if it's only for a little while… I just want to feel something other than fear even if it's just for a few minutes." She'd met his gaze for this first part of her answer, but as she had continued speaking, he watched her eyes lower to his chest as if she were trying to hide the shame she felt by verbalizing her needs.

Trace placed his fingers under her chin, bringing her chin up and waiting until she once again looked into his eyes.

"Thank you for trusting me enough to tell me what you need. I know that was hard for you, and I'm so proud of you for being brave enough to take a chance. I promise you, your trust in me is well placed."

Brushing his lips over hers in soft passes as he smoothed his calloused hands in gentle caresses over the entire length of her back and lush ass, he led her slowly back to the arousal she'd been lost in earlier.

"You are so beautiful, and you have a light that shines from within. When I first saw you sitting out in the snow, I was sure you were a gift sent directly from God, and now? Well, now I'm certain it's true."

As he'd been speaking, he'd been moving his hands in random patterns under the soft shirt. He moved to the hem and slowly drew it over her head, tossing it aside. Leaning back, he let his eyes touch her with the warmth of his appreciation. He knew she'd seen his desire when her nipples tightened even further until they formed the sharpest points he'd ever seen.

"Let me tell you what I see. I see a beautiful woman who has been sold a bill of goods about not being worthy when in reality, any man she gifts with her time, allowing him into her life, should be thanking his lucky stars she has deemed him worthy of her trust. You and I are going to have a long conversation about the lifestyle I embrace, but that is for another time. Right now, I have every intention of giving you exactly what you have asked for, and it is going to be my pleasure to do so. But know this, my lovely snow princess, I am deeply honored you have given me your trust. It's a precious gift, and I want you to know how much it means to me."

Trace moved back over her, holding most of his weight on his elbows, so she would feel him pressing against her without bearing the crush of weight entirely. Her skin almost sparkled in the moonlight shining through the windows high above the bed. Sending up a silent prayer of thanks, Trace was grateful the snow had abated, allowing the moon to kiss Tori's beautiful skin. Even in the low light, he could see how beautifully she was flushing with her arousal.

He moved his knees, so he pushed her thighs apart and shifted just enough to the side, he could run his hand from the side of her face, all the way over her softly rounded breasts, down her belly, then over the curls covering her mound before ever so gently sliding his fingers through her wet folds.

"Oh, princess," he said when a look of embarrassment crossed her face, "you are so wet for me. I am so pleased your body is preparing itself for my possession. My cock is aching to slide deep into your pussy, but I want to know a few things first."

TORI COULD FEEL herself getting lost in the feel of his fingers sliding through her sensitive fold as they lit her up like the Fourth of July.

"I'm on birth control, and I'm clean if those are your questions. I haven't had a man for a very long time, so you may have to go a little slow, at first." Tori was looking everywhere but at him, and she didn't know why it was so hard for her to talk about these things, but it had always had been.

"Well, that does answer a few of my questions. I want you to know, I am also clean. Regular physicals, including testing for disease, are a part of the requirements for membership at ShadowDance." Her confusion must have been reflected in her expression because he shook his head and continued, "I'll tell you all about The Club later. First, I need to know what kind of sexual experience you've had. Have all of your past encounters been vanilla or have you experienced anything that would be considered outside that box?"

She could tell Trace knew the answer the minute he asked the question; she'd only had vanilla sex. Hell, she'd hadn't even had much of that. But she was intrigued by what else was out there, and the heat in his eyes told her he'd sensed her curiosity.

"Well, I... um... I think I know what you are asking, and I've only had regular sex, but I have always wondered... well, about other kinds of sex because I don't seem to be doing the regular stuff quite right because well... because... ummm... well..." *How am I ever going to tell this amazing man I've only had sex twice, and both times were really disappointing for me and for the men I was with.*

"Let's try this, how many men have you had sex with?" He apparently decided it might be easier if he asked direct questions she simply had to answer. And from the intense way he was studying her, she had no doubt he'd be able to fill in most of the blanks just by watching her body language.

"TWO, ONE IN college and one not long after I moved to Houston."

"Very good, princess. Now, how many times did you have sex with your first partner?" Trace was feeling pangs of jealousy, and those were surprising him—a lot!

"Um, well, I only had sex with each of them one time... they didn't seem to think it was an experience worth repeating... if you know what I mean." Her deep sigh of resignation told him volumes about who the asshats had likely blamed for the fact the sex hadn't fulfilled her.

"Tori, did you climax during either of those sexual encounters?" Trace could feel her body tense beneath him and knew the answer before she could answer. He didn't see any reason to make her feel any more humiliation than her partners had already piled on her, so he didn't wait for her response.

"Sweetness, I can tell by your body language, you didn't have an orgasm, and I promise you that drought is going to end tonight. Now, let's see what we can do about letting you fall over the edge of pleasure into a space so filled with warmth and sensation, you will wonder how you've lived without it."

He had been using his voice to draw her in, and he knew from experience, the deep tones of his voice were a powerful tool when seducing a woman. And he had every intention of seducing this one with every single skill he'd learned over the years. Tori deserved an experience she'd be able to remember for the rest of her life because for all intents and purposes, she was a virgin to the pleasures of the flesh. She only needed a tour guide, and he knew every stop along the way.

Yes indeed, the angels had absolutely sent him a very special gift.

TORI WAS EMBARRASSED to her toes she had told the most amazing man she'd ever met about her two very humiliating previous sexual experiences. *Oh yeah, Tori, every man wants to hear about the other men who have fucked you... NOT! Even if they ask, they don't really want to know. What on earth were you thinking?*

Feeling her tension, Trace pulled back from her and looked at her thoughtfully.

"Tell me what just went racing through your thoughts." When her eyes went wide, he continued, "Your body gives you away, princess. Now, out with it." She shuddered at the command in his voice. There was no question the words hadn't been a request, and for some reason, the realization made her pussy liquify rather than contract in fear.

"I was thinking I shouldn't have spoken about the other men. It's tacky, and I can't imagine you really wanted to hear about that. I'm sorry. I really don't know what came over me."

Trace was absolutely captivated by her honesty even as he was mentally mapping out a plan to improve her self-esteem. The pink flush working itself over her satin-soft cheeks was so adorable, he had to fight grinning at her like a fool.

"Well, I asked you, so that means I did want to know.

If we're going to find mutual satisfaction, I need to know about your previous experiences. Without that background information, I'd waste a lot of time with hit-and-miss experimentation, and that is time I would much prefer putting to better use." Sliding his fingers through her folds, he kept talking to her and relished the feel of her body flushing against him with the heat of her arousal. Watching as her entire body turned a beautiful shade of pink was one of the hottest things he'd ever seen.

"I'm going to love watching you come. I can already tell your body is going to sing for me, and I'm going to make sure you sleep like a baby tonight, sweetness." Trace couldn't remember the last time he'd enjoyed touching a woman as much as he was enjoying his time with Tori. And the fact that she was proving to be very responsive was a very pleasant bonus.

Tori closed her eyes and moaned softly. Listening to Trace's words was almost hypnotizing. He continued his verbal assault on her senses.

"First, I'm going to make sure my fingers are well coated with your body's natural lube, then I'm going to tease your clit, drawing it out from its hiding place. When you are close to your first climax, I'm going to pull back because your release will be so much stronger if it is delayed. I'm selfish, and I want my cock deep inside you when you come apart for me the first time."

Tori could feel her heart beating a frenetic tattoo inside her chest, and she was surprised it didn't beat itself right out of her body. She could feel her breathing shift to shallow pants, and she was certain she would be able to come just from listening to Trace describe what he was planning to do to her. The man's voice and hands were pure magic. There was something about their instant connection that drew her to him like a moth to a flame. She couldn't help but worry she was rushing into something without using her head, but at this moment, she just couldn't make her brain work on a level that would support logic or reasoning. Deciding she would worry about it later, she tilted her head back and let the sensations bombarding her take her along for the ride.

TRACE WATCHED AS Tori's mind finally let go, and she finally allowed her body to take over. He always loved that moment with a sub when their minds surrendered into silence and all the little worries and tensions slid to the side until there was nothing left but sensation and feeling racing through their sweet bodies.

The best subs he knew were brilliant men and women who knew the value of getting outside their own heads. Most of those subs described their submission as a chance to let someone else take the reins for a while and just float to a place where they had no responsibility other than to obey the commands and bathe in the ecstasy only a Dom could give them.

Watching a sub slip into that nether land of subspace was the biggest turn-on in the world. Victoria Paulson was obviously a very bright woman and getting her past her own thinking was going to a challenge he'd enjoy.

He was certain she was a natural submissive, but he knew she would likely describe herself as more of a peacekeeper personality. It would be fun to help her explore her curiosity about kink and provide experiences that would help her identify what her particular twist was.

Moving his fingers in a leisurely, random pattern through her slick pussy, he thought one of the first things he would do if she was his sub would be to have her sweet pussy lips waxed, so he'd be able to see each muscle clench and tremor. He loved the feel of a bare pussy, and he would sit her on the coffee table in front of his sofa, spread her legs apart as she leaned back on her elbows. He'd talk to her as he took in the view, watching each and every reaction. Her body would eventually yield all its secrets to him.

Moving his fingers up her torso, he painted her dusty-pink-colored nipples with her juices and sucked the nipple deep into his mouth before pressing the tight bud against the roof of his mouth. God in heaven, she tasted so sweet. Suddenly, he couldn't wait to press his face against her pussy and fuck her with his tongue.

Moving back down her gorgeous body, Trace took his time, mapping her with his mouth and making sure he kissed intricate patterns over her softly rounded belly and hip bones before positioning himself between her legs. She had the most perfect olive-toned complexion he'd ever seen. Her dark eyes and dark skin tone added to her exotic beauty. As soon as Trace plunged his tongue into her pussy, he felt the first telltale tremors of her release, so he pulled back, eliciting a groan of frustration from her.

"You do not have permission to come yet, princess. Don't forget, I told you I want to be fucking you when you come for the first time." This time was just like the last. She reacted immediately to his command. *My snow angel may be the most natural sub I've ever trained.* Trained? Where had that thought come from? He was supposed to be making love to her not thinking about training her. He was trying very hard to stay in the moment, but there was something so basic about their connection, he kept finding his thoughts veering toward the future.

"I'm sorry... I don't know how to stop it... Oh please, I was so close. It just felt like I was being swallowed up by this giant wave and then... and then it was just gone..." Tori's voice was taking on the breathy desperation he loved to reward, so he slowly slid up her body. Hooking his elbows under her knees he pulled her legs up along her sides, so they were parallel to her chest, so wide apart, she was entirely open before him.

"Your body is fucking perfect, and my cock is so hard, I'm afraid this first time may be pretty fast, darlin', but we'll take each other right where we need to go, won't we?" At his last words, he slid just inside her channel and stilled when her muscles clamped down on him like a vise. *Holy shit, this is going to be over before it even starts if you don't get your shit together, Bartell. Christ, she is so tight.*

"Relax your vaginal muscles, Tori, let me in. I'm going to give you the release your body is craving." He could feel her gasp several shallow breaths, trying to align his words with what her body was screaming at her to do. When she finally met his gaze, he could feel her draw strength from him and use it to follow his command.

Slowly, her hot pussy relaxed fractionally, but it was enough to tell him to continue his deep plunge into her without fear he would damage the delicate tissue lining her inner walls. He was surrounded by the most incredible heat, it stole his breath, feeling the subtle rippling and Tori's slick cream against his bare cock. Damn, he hadn't taken a woman bareback since Nan, and the intensity was almost enough to make his head spin.

"That's a good girl. Now, take a deep breath, relax, and let go—let me take you there, princess. Let me make your body sing. Put your hands over your head and hold on to the rails of the headboard. Don't let go until I tell you to, understand?" Having her restrain her own hands would afford her the control he knew she wasn't ready to relinquish yet while also allowing him to see how well she handled a bit of bondage.

When she did as he'd commanded, he felt her vaginal walls quiver as she tried to rein in the urge to shift as she sought her own release. Her respiration was shallow, but the pulse at the base of her neck was beating so fast, he knew she must be feeling the effect of the acceleration. Tori's eyes clouded with desire and need as she struggled to speak.

"Yes. Oh God, please... I... I need you to move. You feel so wonderful inside me. I can feel the ridges and veins of your cock and... oh God, it's so hot inside me... and huge!" That was all it took, Trace began pumping into her with deep plunges alternated with short strokes, varying the speed and intensity to keep her off-balance as long as possible. Her words had taken him by surprise, and he'd lost any pretense of control.

Trace felt the fire in his balls racing up his cock, and just before he sent hot pulsing jets of come against her waiting cervix, he spoke against her ear.

"Come for me, Tori. Let me hear every bit of your pleasure."

TORI HEARD TRACE'S words and felt her body react before her mind had a chance to process what he'd said. She was thrown over the edge into a yawning chasm of bliss that led to what she could only describe as the most amazing vortex of swirling colors imaginable. She heard someone scream his name, and it was a heartbeat or two before she realized it was her own strangled voice she'd heard. When she felt the pulsing of his enormous cock shooting hot jets of cum deep inside her, she vaulted into another soul-shattering orgasm. Feeling him come against her cervix was the very definition of mind-bending bliss.

Trace had thrown back his head and groaned her name as his body was rocked to the core by an orgasm unlike anything he had ever experienced before. On one level, he knew his and Nan's sexual relationship had been wonderful, but this? Oh, good God in Heaven, this was something so much larger than anything he'd ever experienced, it was almost a shock.

For three years, which had felt like thirty, he'd been lost in the depression-fogged memories of a woman he'd loved so deeply, he'd wondered if he would ever love again. And now, the world seemed as if it had just opened itself up in a way he had never anticipated possible. Catching his weight on his arms, he framed her face with his large hands and crashed his mouth to hers. Only their mutual need for oxygen finally forced him to pull his lips from hers.

"Oh, darlin' you rocked my world. That was amazing. I'm going to get a warm, wet cloth. I want you to wait right here." As he stood, he felt his knees start to buckle beneath his weight, and he quickly stiffened them and hurried to bring back a soft cloth. He leaned over Tori's flushed, sated body and gently cleansed their combined juices from her pussy and thighs. He felt her stiffen and pressed a palm against her lower abdomen.

"Shhh, it is my responsibility and privilege to take care

of you. Please, don't deprive me of this pleasure."

Watching Tori immediately relax further demonstrated her naturally submissive nature, and he was momentarily distracted by the sight of her lying spread out before him. She was flushed, limp, sated, and just about the most beautiful sight he'd ever seen. An overwhelming desire to hold her tightly in his heart as well as against his body washed over him like a tsunami.

He cleaned himself with the second cloth and placed them both aside. Getting back into bed, he reached for her and pulled her into his arms, pillowing her sweet face against his shoulder, and smiled as she snuggled against him.

"Princess, you need never worry you aren't doing that right. I think you might have fried a few of my brain cells. If it had been any more *right*, you very likely would have killed me." *But what a way to go.* He smiled at her soft giggle and pulled her even closer.

"Rest now, sweetness." He pressed a kiss to her hair and inhaled the sweet smell of citrus and sage, laced with the intoxicating scent of a well-loved woman. Falling asleep with Tori in his arms felt so right, he let his mind drift into the abyss of pure contentment.

Chapter 4

TRACE WAS AWAKENED twice during the night by Tori's restlessness. He could tell she was struggling on the fringes of a bad dream, and he wondered how long it had been since she'd gotten a decent, uninterrupted night's sleep. Each time, she'd quickly settled when he'd pulled her close and encircled her within his warm embrace, a fact he found immensely satisfying. Just after dawn, he moved carefully to get out of bed without disturbing her. He'd given all the ranch hands the day off—it was Thanksgiving after all—so that meant he was going to be doing all of their chores as well as his own.

Ever since he'd lost Nan, holidays hadn't held any significance for him, but he wanted his men to enjoy their families, and he had always been grateful for the extra work to keep his mind off what he'd lost. Trace hadn't given any thought to what Tori would think of spending Thanksgiving alone. As he sat on the edge of the bed, he felt her stir next to him. When he turned back to her, she was looking at him with sleepy eyes, her hair a mass of disarray, her lips swollen from his kisses, and he didn't think he'd ever seen anyone as beautiful as the sweet snow angel nestled in his rumpled bed.

"Good morning, sweetheart, how did you sleep?" Brushing a few wayward curls from her face, he smoothed the pads of his fingers along the outline of her jaw in a soft caress. He smiled as she leaned into his touch, rubbing her face against his work-roughened palm like a kitten seeking his attention.

She blushed so hot, even the part in her hair turned crimson before she answered, "I slept really well after... well, after we... I mean..." She blew out a soft breath and looked up at him, smiling sweetly.

"Princess, I would like to get one thing cleared up between us, right now." The change in her expression was absolute and shocked him. When she started to move away from him, he caught her, easily halting her retreat.

"Oh no, you don't. You have it all wrong, princess. I just wanted to make sure you know you can say anything to me without feeling embarrassed or intimidated. We have some things to talk about, including the fact I am a Dominant in the bedroom. And, well, that trait often spills over into the rest of my approach to women, but I like to think of it as chivalry outside of this room." He chuckled, and when he gave her a warm smile, she seemed to relax once again. Her trust was like a balm to his aching heart. He knew she'd been convinced he was going to give her the "Last night was a mistake" speech, and he watched as it took a few minutes for his words to fully take root.

"I don't really know anything about that lifestyle. I mean, I have read a few romance novels, but I don't have any personal experience... um... I only have my own curiosity." She'd spoken quietly, but Trace hadn't missed a single word.

"Well, why don't you get up, we'll get something to eat, and I'll see if I can't answer your questions. As a matter of fact, I'd like to ask you some questions as well." When her eyes grew wary, he continued, "I want to learn about the beautiful woman who rocked my world last night, princess, that's all. Please, don't look so frightened every time I say something to you, you're gonna ruin my reputation as a nice guy with that deer-in-the-headlights look." He grabbed her, pulled her onto his lap, and proceeded to kiss her until she'd gone nearly boneless in his arms.

"Now, today is Thanksgiving, but I've given all the men the day off which means I have to cover for them. I'll be grabbing some breakfast, then heading out. I'm going to be covering a lot of the ranch today, and you're welcome to ride along if you're interested." He saw her eyes light up, so he went on, "I'd enjoy the company if you wouldn't mind. I know it's a holiday and all, and we'll be busy until dark, but then I thought we could make a big pot of chili and watch a movie together."

Tori was suddenly struck by the realization she and the gorgeous man before her actually had something in common. They'd both experienced great loss, including having the future they'd thought was all mapped out unexpectedly snatched out of their grasp by circumstances beyond their control. She didn't know the details of his wife's death, he hadn't elaborated much, but she could see flashes of raw grief occasionally in his eyes.

Leaning back, so she could take his face in her hands, she smiled. "Well, Mr. Bartell, I seem to find myself with the holiday free, and I'd love to spend the day with you and get the scenic tour. Do you think you could show me some of the land my uncle left me?" Something flashed in his eyes and for a moment, it was as though Trace cringed, but the look was gone so quickly, she decided she'd imagined it.

"Well, princess, you can use the shower in here or return to the guest suite, whichever appeals to you. I'm going to start a pot of coffee, then I'll shower while you're getting dressed. I think there is bacon in the fridge if you'd like to start it frying when you get finished up here, and I can finish everything up when I get downstairs."

Tori's mind was frantic to find an excuse not to cook. She knew her IQ was well within the gifted range but cooking skills had not only eluded her, they'd never even been in sight. Not a month after she'd moved into the dorm at Harvard, she'd been told if she set off the fire alarms again, she'd be sent packing, and that edict had lasted the entire time she'd lived on campus.

The administration had taken her hot pot and microwave to emphasize their point, and after she'd moved to Houston, her luck in the kitchen had been more of the same. It had been one of her attempts to make her own dinner that led to the fire department being called to her building. Of course, the local police officers always showed up at fire calls. The officer who'd answered the call that night had turned her entire world upside down.

Gradually, she realized she was biting her bottom lip so hard, tears had welled in her eyes and were now making their way down her cheeks as if racing to her chin. Trace had pulled her shaking hands into his and was watching her so closely, it was like he was trying to crawl right inside her thoughts.

"What were you thinking about, Tori? And don't you dare say 'nothing,' or I swear, I'll paddle your sweet ass for lying to me. Now, tell me. I was going to wait until later to start this, but we'll do it now because it's important that I know who put those shadows in your beautiful brown eyes and where I can find the bastard."

Tori was shocked by the possessive growl in his voice,

but she suspected he was every woman's champion, the white knight always rushing to save damsels in distress. Pulling away from him and moving to the window, Tori stood looking out but not really seeing anything. She finally took a deep breath and closed her eyes against the flood of emotions bubbling up inside her.

"I don't even know where to start, and I promise to tell you everything, but I need to get myself settled a bit first." Feeling as if she had just run a marathon, she realized she was wringing her hands so hard, they were turning white. She made a deliberate effort to relax her hands and lay them flat against her sides. Turning to face him, she said, "Let's start with the fact that I can't cook." When he started to speak, she shook her head and forged on.

"No, really. For reasons I can't even begin to explain, everything goes wrong when I try. I'll tell you all the stories some time... honestly, some of them are pretty funny now, and that's saying a lot because they sure weren't funny when they happened. But when you mentioned me starting the bacon, well, that started me thinking about the problems I had in Houston and why you see so little in that piece-of-shit car I was driving. It's such a horribly long story, and I really want that shower and to spend the day with you. Can we just table this discussion for a little while, please?"

She knew her pleading tone was bordering dangerously close to whining, but she was desperate to try to pull back a bit and get her thoughts together. There was just so much about the past several months that was knife-to-the-gut painful, she wasn't sure how to start the conversation, and she knew full well she'd never be able to get through it all in one sitting.

"Okay, that's fair enough," Trace nodded as he stepped

toward her. "No cooking for you until we sort this out." Trace pulled her gently into his arms, hugging her close to his chest, hoping she'd take a moment to soak up a bit of the comfort and relax. *I don't know what's happened to you, sweetheart, but I'm going to do everything I can to help you heal. You deserve a man who will cherish and adore you.* Trace reluctantly released Tori, pulling back to look directly into her sweet face.

"Now, I'm making an executive decision. You'll use this shower because it's better than the one in the guest suite. Make sure you use the massage settings, princess. I want those knots in your shoulders eased by the time you get down to the kitchen. I'll get you something to wear and have everything here on the bed by the time you are ready to dress. Thank you in advance for your trust in me, I just want you to know I'm a very good listener, and I really do want to know what happened in your past."

Turning her around, he placed his hands on her slender shoulders, steered her to the bath, and gave her a gentle push inside before giving her bare ass a gentle swat.

"Inside with you. I'll see you in a little while, and take your time, princess. I want you all sparkly clean and relaxed when you come downstairs." Just as he was about to close the door, he added, "Oh and don't wear anything except what I put out for you. No more and no less, understand?"

Tori could only stare at him and nod. Ordinarily, she would have bristled at such a blatantly controlling remark, but for some reason, it seemed perfectly reasonable coming from the gorgeous man who was looking at her with such unrestrained lust, she was getting goosebumps just from his visual appraisal of her naked body. As he closed the door, the quiet snick of the latch brought her back to the moment, and she set about taking care of business, brushing her teeth with the new toothbrush he'd left on the counter for her, then she opened the door of the shower and gasped at what she found.

The entire bathroom was a stunning contrast of old and new, but the shower was pure decadence. While it was definitely a shower, it reminded her of a small tropical paradise, complete with hanging ferns and a natural rock bench that spanned the entire back wall at different heights. There were multiple showerheads at various levels as well as rain shower faucets suspended high above the open space, so it would be easy to imagine you were actually showering outside in the rain, surrounded by a beautiful forest, blooming flowers, and small waterfalls cresting over jagged rocks along one wall.

The panel that controlled all the elements found inside the enormous enclosure was on the wall just outside the door, and even though it looked like something out of a sci-fi movie, it turned out to be surprisingly user-friendly. Tori even found the music system and quickly discovered she and Trace shared a love for a wide variety of music. She loved the massaging jets and gratefully, let the pulsing water work all the tension out of her back and shoulder muscles. Trace had been right, this was exactly what she needed.

When she exited the shower, Tori found a large fluffy towel on the warming bar. As she patted her heated, flushed skin dry, she sighed at the luxury of being pampered. *Damn, a girl would be totally spoiled in no time around this man.* When she entered the bedroom, wrapped in a robe he had left for her on the marble counter, she stopped abruptly at the sight of a man's white Oxford shirt laid out on the bed.

Assuming he'd left her bra and panties under the shirt, she lifted it as a mixture of apprehension and excitement coursed through her. Tori saw a small note laying alongside the shirt with the words, "No buttons, T" in perfectly printed letters. *Oh Lordy, what have I gotten myself in to?* Smiling to herself, she slipped the soft cotton shirt on over her shoulders and laughed when she noticed it fell easily to the tops of her knees. The lingering scent of Trace's soap and aftershave wrapped around her causing her pussy to flood with moisture. *Get a grip, Tori. You are just setting yourself up again...*

Walking down the stairs, Tori's negative thoughts were scuttled as soon as she breathed in the smell of freshly brewed coffee and bacon frying. When she rounded the corner into the large kitchen, she stopped dead in her tracks. The sight that greeted her stole her breath. She could practically feel her brain cells sizzling right along with the bacon as she watched the way Trace moved. His movements were economical with a natural athletic grace. He was clearly accustomed to working in the kitchen.

She'd noticed how tall he was yesterday when he'd worn his boots, and his height now was not diminished by his bare feet. His softly faded jeans were riding low on lean hips, their bottoms bunched over his feet. The chambray work shirt he wore gaped open with only the middle two buttons holding the placket together. He looked so much more at ease than he had at any time since she'd met him, she caught herself standing and gazing him from the doorway. She was completely mesmerized by his fluid grace. When he looked up at her, she blushed at having been caught staring. She smiled shyly and was rewarded with a blinding grin that gave her a glimpse of the open and honest spirit she was sure was the foundation of the man himself.

"Come to me, princess." His words sent another rush of moisture straight to her pussy, and her feet responded before her mind caught up. "Look at you. You look beautiful in my shirt and nothing else." The corners of his mouth turned up as she felt herself flush. She wasn't used to being complimented, and the sincerity of his words warmed her soul. Pulling her close, he hugged her to his chest for long seconds before brushing kisses over her forehead and the tip of her nose, then sealing his hungry mouth tight over hers.

Holy crap on a cannoli, this man's kiss is lethal. Tori felt her mind start to shut off as she sank further and further into Trace's kiss. She'd never been kissed with the depth of feeling she found herself lost in each time Trace kissed her. It was unnerving how quickly he could take her so completely off her train of thought.

"HAVE A SEAT when you're ready, breakfast is almost finished. Coffee is over there, and juice is in the fridge, princess. Please make yourself at home." He quickly filled their plates and placed them on the small table in front of a bank of windows looking out over a backyard that was a virtual winter wonderland. At her quiet gasp, he followed her line of sight and smiled.

"Beautiful isn't it? The snow fell so level, even the rails of the fences are covered this morning. We get a lot of snow each year, but the first one is always my favorite." He laughed softly and added, "Of course by the time spring finally rolls around, we're all very happy to see the last of it melt away."

Looking over at her soft features, he was struck by the look of wonder on her heart-shaped face, and when he returned his gaze to the windows. He tried to view it through her eyes, and somewhere, in the back of his mind, he noted how good it felt to care enough about a woman again to want to make that effort. Turning back to the table, he took her hand in his and guided her to a seat.

"Come on, sweetness. Let's eat while it's still hot, then I'll let you change into something warmer before we set out. But for now, let me show you how I'd like you to sit for me during our meal." After he'd shown her how to hook her feet on the outside of the legs of her chair, so she was open to his touch, he smiled as her face went crimson again. *God, love a woman who is still innocent enough to blush.* "I love touching you, pet, and just knowing you are open for that touch pleases me more than I can tell you."

He knew Tori's mind was reeling, she probably didn't understand why everything that was happening turned her on when society had taught her she should be protesting his highhanded ways. After all, why would an independent, intelligent woman become soaking wet from handing over so much power to a man? He'd heard more than one sub describe it as baffling in the beginning, and he almost laughed out loud when he heard her mutter something about the reptilian part of her brain must be the only section working.

Trace watched Tori closely as she struggled with all the issues that typically plagued submissives in the early stages of their introduction to the lifestyle. In this day and age, it was always so difficult for women, in particular, to under-stand that even though they submitted sexually, they still retained all the power.

The two of them enjoyed a companionable silence as they ate, and Trace was impressed she wasn't hell-bent on filling the peaceful quiet. Trace was fully aware of the difference in their sizes and was relieved she didn't seem intimidated.

"Thank you for breakfast. It was delicious." She picked up their plates and headed to the sink before she continued, "You cooked, so I'll clean up." It didn't take her any time at all to set the kitchen back to rights, and she noticed he just leaned back in his chair, his long legs stretched out in front of him, watching her as interest and something else she couldn't quite identify sparkled in his intelligent eyes.

THEY SPENT THE entire day checking cattle, making sure water supplies were open, and each pasture they visited had plenty of hay set in the feeders. They'd laughed at the antics of the calves as they ran in groups, reminding her of mini-stampedes, but Trace had said it was more likely they should be compared to gangs of unruly teens, looking for mischief to get into.

Tori had been surprised at how loud the little hellions had been as they'd run from one end of the pasture to the other, and she giggled when they'd kicked up their heels, obviously relishing the crisp mountain air. She had enjoyed seeing the land her uncle had left her and was relieved to know Trace was the rancher she'd been told was currently leasing the pastures. She didn't have any intention of buying or managing cattle and confessed she hadn't really given much thought to what she would do with the land.

"What do you think I should do with the land?" she

asked, sensing his tension. "I don't know anything about ranching, and since there isn't a place to live out here..." She let her words trail off as she got lost in the thoughts racing through her mind. When she was finally able to continue, she simply said, "I thought I could stay here for a while, that I'd be safe here."

Coming back to the moment, she realized Trace had stopped the truck and was turned toward the passenger side of the truck, watching her intently, his concern clearly reflected in his compassionate expression. She hadn't even realized she was crying until he reached over and wiped the tears from her cheeks with the pads of his thumbs.

"Talk to me, Tori... what are you running from?" When he saw her muscles visibly tense, he pulled her into a hug and just held her for long minutes, giving her a chance to center her thoughts before setting her back in her seat again, so he could look into her eyes.

Tori didn't start talking for a few seconds, then the words seemed to tumble out faster and faster until she'd told him all about moving to Houston, the fire department's visit to her condo, and how the officer she'd met that night had taken an interest in her and asked her out to dinner. She told him how she'd known early on during that first date, Officer Gary George wasn't someone she would be interested in seeing again, and when he'd sensed her withdrawal, he had started pressuring her about returning to her place for drinks and telling her where they'd be going the next night.

Thinking back on all the things Gary George had done to her during the past year, she wondered again if she had finally managed to elude him or if this was just the calm before another storm. He'd destroyed the few keepsakes she'd managed to save from her mother, killed her dog, and ruined several cars. But the worst thing he'd managed to do was alienate her from her friends and co-workers.

Tori had needed to stop several times while she was telling her story to regroup, and she was grateful for Trace's patience. He never tried to rush her, his questions quiet and thoughtful, just enough to let her know he was actively listening. A couple of times, she noted something in his demeanor that seemed to radiate anger, but she knew it wasn't directed at her, and he was able to mask it quickly. When she'd finally purged herself of almost all the disgusting details, she sagged in her seat, feeling like a marionette whose strings had been suddenly severed by the puppet master. Looking up into his eyes, her words sounded thin and exhausted even to her own ears.

"I'm sorry, I shouldn't have just unloaded all that septic information on you like that. But it's just that it's been... well, it's been a rough year and you are the first person who has really listened... and I well, I guess I..."

"Stop!" His quiet command might have been spoken in a soft voice, but there was no doubt it was meant to bring about her silence. "Princess, don't you dare apologize for doing exactly what I asked you to do. You should never feel any guilt for sharing information that's vital to your health or safety... and I do mean *not ever*! Hear this and hold these words close to your heart as you get to know me and the other people in Climax—we take care of and fiercely protect what belongs to us. We take great pride in keeping our women and children safe, and I'm sure some people will insist, we're practically obsessive about it."

His smile took away some of the sharpness of his words, letting her know he wasn't trying to frighten her. "I'll introduce you to Katarina, Jenna, and Rissa, they'll all tell you how serious we are about the safety of all the women in our close-knit community."

He took her small hand in his and leisurely drew circles slowly over her palm as he spoke. She marveled at how soothing the small gesture was and how grateful she was he wasn't pressing her for more information.

"You're safe here, Tori, I want you to know that, and if your stalker cop shows up, I'll keep you safe." He paused for so long, she wasn't sure he was going to continue, but he finally added, "I think you should consider staying at the ranch until you are sure he didn't track you here. Alex and Zach have considerable resources and contacts, and I'd like to ask them to check this out, so you can safely put it all behind you. What do you say?"

Tori was terrified Gary might find a way to track her. Even though she'd taken every precaution she could, in the end, she knew how difficult it was to truly disappear, particularly when her inheritance in Colorado was public record. He'd find it, eventually, if he was really looking.

Gazing out the window of his large truck, she wanted nothing more than to just curl up and sleep. It had always been her escape of choice when she was stressed, and she could feel the fatigue overtaking her as the minutes ticked by.

"That's probably a good idea," she finally nodded. "I have been worried he might be looking for me. The night he killed Duchess and left her battered body on my porch, he told me he would never let me go, that I'd end up just like my 'fucking dog' if I ever let another man touch me."

TRACE COULDN'T REMEMBER ever being as angry as he was

at that moment. It took every ounce of control he possessed to push it back, but he did because it wasn't what his snow princess needed. Tori needed tenderness and to be wrapped in the shelter of his protection without feeling the rage vibrating through him with seismic intensity. He pulled her against his chest and just held her while she fell into quiet sobs once again.

"Shhh... princess, you have to stop, you are going to make yourself sick. Come on now. Let's get you back to the ranch. I'll make us some kick-ass chili while you take a relaxing bath, and when you're done, we'll drink some wine, eat our chili, and watch television. Come on now, I want you to get those tears out, but you need to pace yourself, sweetness."

He settled her back in her seat and leaned across her to draw her seat belt back into place, brushing a soft kiss over her tear-stained cheeks as he did.

"You are so incredibly brave, and I'm so proud of you. I'll make a few calls while you enjoy the hot tub in the master bath, then we'll see if we can't polish off a bottle of wine and enjoy the rest of our day." Brushing the damp curls back from her face, Trace threaded his fingers in her hair, anchoring her gaze to his.

"I want you to know this is the first year since my wife died that I don't have to use my imagination to find something to be thankful for because you're right here in front of me. I'm so very thankful I found you sitting on that snowy bench." Brushing the pads of his thumbs over her tear-stained cheeks, he looked into her eyes for several seconds. "You're so beautiful. Happy Thanksgiving, my sweet snow angel."

Chapter 5

A FTER THEY'D MADE their way back to the ranch house, Trace made sure Tori had everything she needed, then quickly moved downstairs to set the chili on the stove to warm before grabbing his cellphone, so he could talk while he threw together everything else for their dinner.

He called the Lamonts first, knowing their security staff at The Club would have computer access mere mortals could only dream about. After he'd finished explaining the situation to Alex and Zach, they promised to get their team on it right away and agreed to notify Dylan Marshall, the local sheriff as well.

Dylan and his new wife were both former DEA agents who'd maintained many of their federal contacts after leaving the agency, so their resources were widespread and reliable. Both Alex and Zach and several members of the ShadowDance staff were former Special Forces soldiers, but Trace was sure it would be their resident computer genius, Mitch Grayson who would be able to ferret out everything there was to know about Officer Gary George of the Houston Police Department. There was little doubt, in just a few hours, Mitch would have a file on George that would make the FBI envious and the CIA proud.

Trace had a huge amount of respect for his friends and felt humbled at how quickly they were rallying around

Tori—a woman they hadn't even met yet. Satisfied he'd set the wheels in motion, he slipped upstairs to take a fast shower and was heading back down when he heard soft sobbing from the guest room. When he opened the door, he saw Tori sitting on the floor with her small suitcase opened in front of her. Kneeling down beside her, he ran his fingers through her wet hair.

"What's wrong, princess?"

"It's just so incredibly sad. I worked so hard. Hell, I worked two jobs all through college even while I was in law school. I saved so much money, I was able to move without incurring any debt. Damn it, I didn't even have any student loans. When I got to Houston, I was very careful, only buying quality clothes that would hold up to the demands of my career, and in the end, I had to leave so quickly, this is all I have to show for all those years of hard work. I don't know what I'll do now. If I apply to transfer my license to another state, I know he'll find me before I'd even be able to set up a practice or get a job." Taking a deep breath, she looked up at him and smiled weakly.

"My God, I'm such a train wreck, and I'm sure you are tired of hearing me whine. So..." Trace watched as she seemed to draw herself up, taking a couple of steadying breaths, trying to regain her composure. He watched her as she seemed to literally pull a shield up around herself. "I'm going to stop complaining and just accept the fact I have to do whatever it takes. I've built a life from ashes before, and I can do it again."

Trace scooped her up off the floor and moved confidently to the small chaise lounge in front of a large bank of windows. Settling her on his lap, so she faced him, he frowned.

"This is your last reminder, princess. Don't you ever

dare apologize for how you feel. You humble me with your honesty and courage. Knowing you trust me enough to share your feelings and frustrations pleases me more than I can tell you. Please remember that as we discuss things later tonight because trust is going to be the most basic element in the conversation we're going to have, all right?" He waited until he saw a flicker of anticipation in her dark chocolate eyes.

"I want you to remember, clothing can be replaced... *you cannot*. You are safe because you were smart and resourceful. I've already made some calls, and as we speak, there are several people gathering information for us. By this time tomorrow, we'll know more about the asshole who terrorized you than he knows about himself."

Smiling at her surprised expression, Trace set her on her feet, moved to her suitcase, pulled out a pair of yoga pants and a clingy crop top, and handed them to her.

"Put these on and nothing else." Smiling when her jaw dropped open, he put his fingers under her chin and pushed it closed before he continued, "No, no underwear. You won't be needing them this evening. If your feet get cold, feel free to put on a pair of socks, but that is all you'll need. Now put them on quickly, and we'll go downstairs together. You're in for a treat, princess. Dinner should be ready, and I make a mean bowl of chili and a tasty salad if I do say so myself."

TORI COULDN'T REMEMBER ever enjoying a meal more than she had the fresh salad, chili, and crackers she shared with Trace as they watched football on television. He'd been thrilled to find out she was a football fan, and they'd jeered and cheered their favorite teams through two bowls of chili each while they knocked back two bottles of the best wine Tori had ever enjoyed. By the time the games had concluded, they were both enjoying the full effects of the wine and each other's company.

Trace wedged himself into the corner of the large sectional and pulled Tori's back flush against his chest, settling her lush ass between his legs. It was a position he sometimes used for discussions with subs because he could feel every flex of the muscles and intake of breath as well as monitor changes in their pulse rate.

He'd also discovered it often enabled a submissive to answer questions more honestly if they didn't have to look directly at the Dom demanding answers. The small measure of distance seemed to afford them a certain amount of anonymity and therefore, freed them to open up in ways they might not have otherwise.

After a few minutes of just holding her close and enjoying the feel of her against his cock, he nuzzled close to her ear, outlining the shell with his tongue.

"Princess, tell me what you know about Dominants and submissives." He knew instantly she had some frame of reference by the immediate tensing of her muscles, so he added, "I want to remind you of the importance of honesty, darlin'. You should know that your body language has already given you away. I would also like to know whether or not any of your experience is from firsthand exposure or if it's all from reading and research." He knew she was rattled and frantically trying to figure out how to word her answer just right, and he had to smile. *Always the counselor. Well, Ms. Attorney, I'll just wait you out.*

TORI WAS REELING. She was afraid if she told Trace she'd always harbored a deep curiosity about the D/s lifestyle, he'd think she was some kind of freak or worse yet, that she had done something to deserve the pain she'd suffered at the hands of her stalker. Finally, deciding she was tired of being afraid of her own shadow, she answered.

"Um… well, I've read about it, a lot about it, actually, but I don't have any personal experience. Please don't think badly of me, but I've read some books that were on the edgy side… and well, that's where I learned about it."

Trace had been a Dom for years and had a well-developed a very keen sense of listening skills, and what he'd just heard was Tori's admission to a solid curiosity about the lifestyle. *Perfect! Now, my precious little sub, I can tell there is more. You might as well spill it because I'll stay at you until I know everything.* He decided to wait her out, sure she would continue talking if he didn't rush her, and time was on his side. His patience was rewarded when she sighed before finally continuing.

"I went to a club once in Houston, just to see if what I was reading was true." Trace noted how her pulse spiked, and her breathing became little more than shallow panting. "It wasn't anything like what I expected, it was so scary, and strange men and women kept coming up to me and touching me. I paid a large cover charge, and I was only there about twenty minutes. One man demanded I strip and suck his… well, you know. I ran out and never went back." The shiver that raced up her spine radiated out from her core and didn't end until it reached her fingers and toes, and Trace felt each tremble.

Tori remembered the abject terror she'd felt as strange men and women had tried to touch her intimately. She'd been terrified the entire time she'd been inside the filthy warehouse which had been converted into the only club she'd been able to find that allowed admittance by paying the hefty cover charge. Every other club she'd found required extensive background screenings and waiting periods, and she had been sure she would lose her nerve or that discovery would ruin her fledgling career, so she'd opted for the quick look-see that had turned out to be one of her dimmer moments.

TRACE HAD HEARD enough. Shifting her around, so they were face-to-face, he began by assuring her all the reasons her curiosity was perfectly acceptable. He'd quickly added that willing stepping into a situation of which you have little or no knowledge or control is not acceptable—ever.

"First of all, let me assure you that your curiosity is completely normal, and you should never let anyone make you feel it isn't or that you are *less* because you are seeking a way to fulfill yourself. There is no right or wrong in consensual sex." He took her small hands between his larger ones and held them securely before continuing.

"Now, let's talk about the fact you are a beautiful woman who went into an unknown sex club alone without doing any research about the establishment, its members, rules, safety measures, etc. I am known as a very gentle Dom because I'm tolerant and dislike physical pain as punishment unless it's absolutely necessary. But if you were mine and you put yourself in that kind of danger, you would find yourself over my knee the instant I discovered what you'd done. I'd paddle your sweet ass until I was convinced you would never endanger yourself in such a careless way again."

Tori gasped in surprise and tried to pull her hands from his, and even though he knew she was shocked by his words, he was convinced she was even more shocked by her reaction to them. He'd no more than spoken the words when he smelled the sweet scent as her arousal as her pussy flooded with liquid heat.

She'd never had a man care enough to demand she take care of herself, and he intended to see that wrong set to right. Trace watched the sweet sub in front of him as her pupils dilated, and he smiled to himself, knowing she'd become aroused when he'd spoken of spanking her for putting herself in a dangerous situation. When she had tried to pull back, and he'd tightened his hold as a test of how she reacted to that small bit of restraint, he'd been pleased to see her eyes immediately drop to her lap. Her pulse and respiration rates had shifted upward. *Oh yeah...princess, you are fucking perfect.*

"Stop over thinking this, Tori, and let me tell you what I see. I see a gorgeous woman who has had to work hard to put herself through college and establish herself in a career that is highly stressful. I see a very attractive and intelligent woman who understands the world still judges women based on their looks, and despite the fact she is brilliant, many people don't even look beyond the surface. Most people don't take into account the desires and needs of the passionate woman underneath. I see a woman who is a submissive but who doesn't understand the true meaning of the word in the BDSM world. I see a woman who is frightened of being judged and who now faces a danger that is beyond her ability to control, so she's run, and I thank God she ran to Climax where she'll be safe and protected. I see a woman who now has the opportunity to explore her sexuality, both here and at ShadowDance where the guidelines all revolve around the tenant 'Safe, Sane, and Consensual.' I see a woman who sparks a fire in me I was afraid would never be rekindled."

Tori felt shaken to her core by his words. How had this man seen so much in such a short time? When she looked up, tears filled her eyes because it felt as if he'd stripped away so many layers she kept wrapped tightly around herself to protect her fragile self-esteem. She was unsure how to respond. When she looked down again, Trace used a finger to lift her chin again and ran his thumb over her lower lip.

"Princess, tell me what you think being a submissive means." Tori was torn between telling him she already knew she was likely a sub but didn't want to be or lying and just rattling off nonsense.

"And let me be clear about something, Tori, I expect you to answer me honestly. Lying, and that includes lying by omission, is not something I will tolerate."

TRACE CRINGED AS he spoke the words because it struck him that he was a hypocrite of the highest order. Hell, he still hadn't told her about all his offers to buy her uncle's land—*Shit!* He promised himself he would remedy that as soon as possible, but right now, he needed to concentrate on making sure Tori understood exactly what she would gain by indulging her curiosity.

He watched as she worried her lower lip, and he practically could hear the thoughts racing through her mind. He hoped she'd opt for the truth because he didn't want to have to back up his promise of punishment—that wasn't the way he wanted to start with her, but he would if he was forced to. After all, any failure to follow through would be a violation of trust.

If a Dom told a sub of a consequence, he had to follow through, no matter how much he or she didn't want to. *Oh, sweetheart, don't lie to me, please. I would so much rather your first spanking was erotic and not a punishment. I can't wait to watch your beautiful ass turn a nice warm pink under my hand.*

Staying in control was essential early in their bonding as Dom and sub, and it was taking everything he had to wait her out. He was startled by how important it had become to make her his, but even that realization wasn't enough to make him stray from a lifelong belief you should always begin as you intended to go.

TORI COULD FEEL her heart beating so hard, she was worried it would rattle right out of her chest. She was aroused and scared at the same time. Gary George had frightened her more times than she wanted to remember, but this wasn't that kind of fear. This was a fear of finding something within herself she'd never expected, and for some reason, she was terrified of letting Trace down despite the fact it wasn't logical because they'd only just met.

"Um… well, I… damn this is so much harder than I thought it would be."

"No, it is actually very easy if you will just answer without trying to edit. I assure you, you won't shock me, you won't tell me anything that will change the way I see you." Trace still held her hands in his as he spoke, but his hold was no longer restraining, rather the touch was meant to focus her attention on him rather than on her own insecurities. Tori finally took a deep cleansing breath and spoke with a strong voice.

"I have read some about Ds relationships and scenes, and I, well, I suspected I was a sub, well, maybe a little more than suspected. But anyway, I was curious about it… and… well, it seemed like it turned me on when I read stories. But, well, I'm really scared to think about some things, and I don't want to give up my independence, and I'm scared of being hurt. And well… I guess I just never want to be weak. If I give up all the control, then someone else is the strong one, and I'm used to having to be strong and well… um… well, sometimes I like to be on top." She'd said the last part of the sentence so quietly, he almost missed it.

Keeping her hands enfolded in his, Trace looked into her eyes and thought for a minute he might fall into their dark depths.

"Princess, when you meet the subs at ShadowDance, you are going to meet some of the strongest women I've ever met. We'll go to dinner there this weekend before attending a Club night, and it will give you a chance to get to know some of the women I'm talking about. But I want to make it crystal clear that giving up control, letting go of all the expectations and just trusting your Dom will give you everything you need sexually requires a lot more strength than you know, and best of all, it allows the sub to just let go and enjoy. You won't have to worry about anything except following directions. Your only responsibility is immediate compliance." His raised eyebrow stopped her when she would have argued.

"No, it's true. I'll bet your vanilla sexual experiences have been filled with you having complete conversations with yourself in your head wondering if you should do this or should do that. I'll also wager you have been so lost in your worries about whether or not you were doing something right or wrong, you felt like your body was never going to find the sweet release it craved, and ultimately, you were left feeling bereft." Tori appeared mesmerized by the accuracy of his description, so he continued.

"I'd also guess your partners blamed you for your lack of release, claiming you were frigid or incapable of orgasm. Or worse, they pushed you until you felt obligated to fake a response. Did I get it about right?"

Trace knew he had nailed it because he'd seen it too many times and heard about it from other Doms just as frequently. Added to the fact her jaw had been hanging open the whole time he'd been speaking, well, it didn't exactly take a genius to figure this one out. He knew his assessment of things was accurate, but he'd have never predicted her reaction. He was shocked to the tips of his toes when she leaned her head back and laughed so hard, she had tears running down her cheeks before she managed to get herself back under control.

Chapter 6

TRACE DIDN'T REMEMBER the last time a sub's reaction had so completely blindsided him. He just sat and stared at her the entire time as she laughed hysterically. When she finally settled, he regained his composure enough to say, "Well, I have to tell you, that reaction didn't do much for my ego, princess. Want to tell me why you found my take on your situation so damned funny?"

Tori knew immediately she had offended him, and she sobered and apologized. "I'm really sorry. I swear I wasn't laughing at you, well, not directly." At his raised-eyebrow, she quickly continued, "I was laughing because you were so terribly spot-on, that I wondered if someone had sent out a memo or something. It's kind of humiliating when the most handsome and interesting man you have ever met knows how sexually inept you are. I mean, think about it, I've told you about the books I've read and my trip to that nasty-assed club in Houston, and you know every sorry secret of my lame sex life… and, well, it's just so incredibly pathetic. Christ, is there a sign above my head that says, 'Sex Loser'? God, I haven't even had sex for four years because it was so degrading." Suddenly her laughter turned to sobs, and Trace pulled her into his arms and let her vent all her pent-up frustration.

Most of her continued railing as she cried didn't make

sense—hell, some of it was completely incoherent—but the bits and pieces he'd caught were self-depreciating enough, he finally called a halt to it.

"All right, that's enough. I won't allow you to degrade yourself. I would much rather we use that energy to get you to the release your body has been craving for entirely too long." When she finally offered a small, tentative smile, he asked her simply, "Do you trust me?"

Watching her eyes go from curiosity to worry to desire in less than a couple of heartbeats was fascinating. He waited and watched as she tried to organize her thoughts. She was obviously torn between her desire and her fear.

He could see the tug-of-war taking place, but she had to make this decision on her own without his influence. He could take her places sexually she'd never even imagined existed if she would just give them both the opportunity. But until she was willing to admit to her body's needs, there wasn't anything he could do but wait her out.

TORI WANTED TO agree, but she was so scared. Oh, she wasn't frightened of Trace, quite the opposite actually. She was scared she wouldn't be enough for him. What if those two guys in college were right, what if she was frigid? Oh damn, she felt just like she had when she'd tried skydiving. This was just like standing in the door of the plane, trying to gather her courage to take that small step out, trusting her parachute was going to carry her safely where she needed to go. Did she believe Trace would pack her parachute correctly?

"Yes, I trust you." *I don't really understand why, but I*

know you would never intentionally hurt me. She watched as Trace released a breath she doubted he realized he'd been holding.

"Princess, I want you to know, I am very pleased you trust me. I'll do everything in my power to make sure you know your trust is always valued and honored. Before we go any further, I want to tell you something that you need to be aware of." She knew her expression had suddenly become guarded, and he shook his head slightly.

"No, it's nothing bad, but I can't in good conscience tell you to be completely honest if I'm not willing to do the same." Again, there was a part of her that wanted to pull back from him, but he held her close. "This is about your uncle's land, Tori. I just want you to know that I tried several times to get him to sell it to me. I knew his health was failing, and I'd always kept a lookout for him and knew he needed the money. It frustrated me that he lived in that old house when I knew he would have been able to live out his last years in comfort if he'd been willing to sell. He wasn't interested, and he continually insisted it was going to bring his family home to a place they needed to be."

She felt her mouth drop open, and he just smiled at her.

"I'm starting to think he was a pretty fair prophet because that land brought you to Climax, and I'm mighty grateful it did." Trace could tell Tori was carefully considering everything he'd just told her, but he was surprised at her next words.

"Is that it? Just that you tried to buy the land… that's all?" She looked as if she couldn't believe he had found that so important, he had to mention it or she might think he was dishonest.

Taking a deep breath, he answered, "The day we met, I

was in town to meet with Victor Paulson to try to and persuade him, you, to sell. You see, the land isn't really worth much to anyone but me because of access and water. After we met, and I found out who you were, I should have told you right away. I feel bad I didn't do that. It's not like me to be secretive. You had a right to know, but honestly, I was just so blown away by my attraction to you, I didn't want to risk you running in the other direction. And, sweetheart, you needed a friend just as much as I've needed one these past two years."

When Tori told him she'd never met anyone with a higher level of integrity, it touched him deeply. She added, "Thank you for telling me, but it really isn't a problem. It is only reasonable you would try to buy land that borders your ranch. I was relieved to know you were the one using the land. I'm really over my head here and knowing I'm dealing with someone I trust is a huge comfort."

"I have rented the grass for years, and as you know, those were my cattle in the pasture. Your uncle was a stubborn man, and he wouldn't let me raise the rent when it should have gone up a long time ago. He insisted he liked helping out a 'young rancher just getting started.' Well, that rent needs to go up significantly, and we'll be discussing that if you decided you want to keep the land. I won't pressure you to do anything. Whether you sell or keep it is completely up to you. But if you do keep it, I am going to insist you accept more rent."

Tori knew at that moment, she had found a community to call home. She would likely sell the land to Trace because she'd like to buy a small house in town and set up a practice nearby.

"Do you think there would be enough business here for another attorney? I mean, I don't want to take anyone's clients or step on any toes or anything, but…"

Now it was Trace's turn to laugh out loud, interrupting her. At her surprised look, he said, "Oh, princess, when old man Sherman hears you are interested in setting up here, he is going to be thrilled. He has only stayed on because he didn't want to leave the town without a lawyer. I'll get word to him right away. It'll make his holiday so much sweeter. He will probably walk out of his office and never look back as he hands you the key at the door."

His sincerity warmed Tori's heart, and she couldn't believe an elderly uncle she'd never met had foreseen her need for this place and these people, but now, she was even more grateful for his generous gift. Trace brought her back to the moment when he continued.

"All that aside, I believe we have some unfinished business between us. And I think we need to return to that now." He had to hold back his smile as he watched her react to his changed tone. He'd used his Dom voice and was pleased to see her respond so quickly.

"You please me so much, Victoria. I can't tell you how much I enjoy watching your nipples peak and show themselves through the thin fabric of your tank top. And I really like watching the way your skin reacts when I do this." Trace lightly drew his finger across the narrow expanse of exposed skin between the bottom of her skimpy shirt and the top of her low-slung yoga pants.

"Princess, watching the changes in your breathing and pulse makes me so hard, it is almost painful." He smiled just enough to take the edge off her anxiety. "Now, stand in front of me, sweetheart." When she positioned where he wanted her, he crossed his arms over his chest and studied her for long seconds waiting until she was fidgeting. *Perfect.*

"Strip."

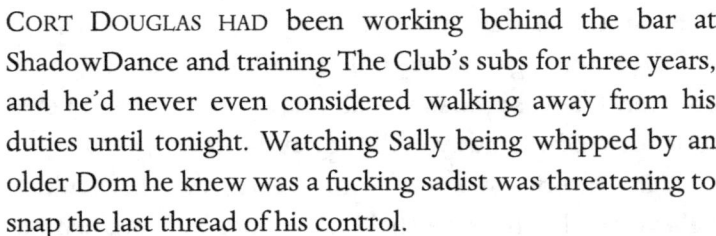

CORT DOUGLAS HAD been working behind the bar at ShadowDance and training The Club's subs for three years, and he'd never even considered walking away from his duties until tonight. Watching Sally being whipped by an older Dom he knew was a fucking sadist was threatening to snap the last thread of his control.

He'd been attracted to Sally the entire time he'd known her but had found excuse after lame excuse to not act on his feelings. And now, he was left watching as the man using a single-tail whip on her left marks all over her back and thighs. She'd been gagged and was tied to a St. Andrew's cross. He could see her face in the large mirror mounted behind the small raised stage.

He'd only met her gaze once, and she'd quickly looked down as if ashamed to find herself in such a situation which he found odd. When she finally looked up again, he saw her pleading expression and immediately launched himself over the bar moving quickly to the scene area.

"Stop! I am uncertain about this sub's well-being." His sharp words caused the Dom to look up, and Cort knew immediately the man was so lost in Dom space, he wasn't even tracking the condition of the woman he was whip-ping.

"Get out of my scene. If you weren't so overindulgent in your treatment of the subs you are training, Doms like me wouldn't have to pick up the slack and whip them into shape." The man's words and crazed expression caused a crowd to gather and quickly caught the attention of Club owners, Alex and Zach Lamont. Alex moved quickly to stand at Cort's side.

"What's going on here?" Looking at his longtime friend and employee, he said, "Cort, I assume you have a good reason for interrupting this scene?" Alex and Zach both knew about Cort and Sally's mutual interest and had wondered how to provide them with a gentle push toward each other. It looked like they might have just been handed the perfect opportunity.

"Of course, I know this submissive well. I trained her, and I know her tolerance levels. I believe this scene has exceeded those. I'd like to check with her to make sure she is in the right frame of mind to call a halt if it's too much for her." He turned to the Dom who was still flipping the whip nervously with small movements. "What is her safe-word signal?"

"Fuck that, she doesn't need a damned signal. She needs this punishment after she turned me down last weekend." The Dom's eyes were glazed over, and he all but shouting in his frustration.

Zach had moved to Sally and was removing the gag from her mouth by the time Cort turned to face her. Zach leaned forward and used a small towel to wipe her face and spoke in a firm but compassionate voice.

"Sally, talk to me. Did you enter into this scene of your own free will without a safe-word signal?" Zach couldn't imagine the woman putting herself in any position of danger because she had a young child to care for, and he knew Sally's little girl was the center of her world. She had worked for The Club for over a year and had never shown any tendency toward reckless behavior before.

Sally's eyes flicked to Cort, then refocused on Zach before she answered.

"No, Sir, I did not. I would never do anything so dangerous. I didn't even want a scene with..." Cort watched the tears start falling and began removing the unlined leather cuffs the prick had placed on her delicate wrists and ankles. Pressing his fingers to her lips, he stopped her from finishing what she was saying, knowing she needed care more than they needed answers right at this moment.

Zach's voice calmed her as he spoke softly. "Shhh, that's enough for now. We'll get you settled and taken care of while Master Alex and I have a chat with Master Jacobs in our office." Alex was already escorting the man from the room for what Cort knew would be the last time. His membership was about to be revoked for life; no one tricked a sub at ShadowDance or hurt one purposely because he or she had refused a previous scene. *What part of consensual had escaped this asshole's attention?*

The bastard would be banned from not only this establishment but every other one in their network as well. The ShadowDance Club would send his picture and a summary of what happened to nearly three hundred fetish clubs across the United States and Canada, essentially blackballing him from every major club in both countries. There wasn't any guarantee the son-of-a-bitch wouldn't ever hurt another sub, but they could make sure he didn't have easy access to them.

Cort stepped up, placing his hands on both sides of her face as Zach and the dungeon monitor finished releasing the cuffs cutting into her abraded wrists and ankles. She was quickly wrapped securely in one of the soft subbie blankets used for aftercare. Cort scooped her up in his arms and headed for a small alcove that was shielded from view by large plants. The area was fairly private, and the small alcove was often used by Doms when their subs needed a

bit more privacy when coming back down after a particularly intense scene.

Zach put his hand on Cort's shoulder as he'd walked
away and told him they would cover the bar for the rest of
the evening. Zach knew it was more important for Cort to
take care of his woman, and he hoped like hell Cort came
to his senses and realized what a perfect match he and Sally
were before she gave up and moved on.

Chapter 7

T RACE WATCHED AS Tori fought the internal battle all subs fight in the beginning—the tug-of-war of emotions, see-sawing between the desire to submit and explore the needs she felt simmering inside versus the ingrained need to be independent.

Slowly, her fingers found the hem of her shirt and pulled it over her head, sending her hair cascading over her shoulders in beautiful waves of shiny silk. After carefully folding the shirt and setting it aside, she hooked her thumbs into the waistband of her yoga pants and peeled them slowly down her thighs in a move that was pure poetry in motion.

"Very nice, princess, you have pleased me with your obedience. Now move your feet shoulder width apart and leave your arms at your sides. No matter what I do, don't move your feet." He knew there was no possible way she would be able to stay completely still. It was a given she'd move, the only question being how long she'd be able to hold on. Standing behind her, he moved his hands slowly over her shoulders, smoothing them down her arms all the way to her fingertips, leaning over her shoulder, so she would be able to feel his breath on her ear.

"You are so beautiful, like a gift straight from God. A special delivery set right into my very grateful hands."

TORI WAS SURE Trace could feel the small tremors racing through her body. His large, calloused hands felt as if they were sparking small electric shocks through her body, and all those powerful flickers were gathering in her now soaking wet sex. *Oh. My. Heavenly. God. What he does to me. Just being near him makes me feel like I've been plugged into electricity. I don't know how I'll ever be able to stand still when I can already feel my knees wobbling. It'll be so damned embarrassing when I collapse in a heap on the floor.*

"Shhh. I promise, I won't let you fall." Trace's words shocked her, and she knew she'd spoken the words aloud rather than just letting them float through her wandering thoughts. "You are safe with me in all ways, princess. When you submit to a Dom, it should be with everything in you. If you can do that for me, I'll take you to a sexual plane you have never even imagined exists." He moved his hands to her back, long strokes from her shoulders to the dip at the top of her ass. This was a man who knew the power of touch, and the lowest part of her back was a hot spot for her. She practically melted against him and heard his satisfied chuckle.

"I see holding completely still is going to be something we'll need to work on. For now, we'll just worry about your feet. Remember, you do not have permission to move them, princess."

Yeah, good luck with that. It only took a few strokes before she was arching her back, pushing her ass out, seeking his touch as hands brushed lowered.

"I'm thrilled with your response to my hands skimming their way over your beautiful body, Tori. Knowing you are seeking my touch calls to me in a way I can't describe. Resting my hand just a breath above your ass as we move through a crowded room or weave our way between tables in a restaurant represents a level of intimacy I'm looking forward to sharing with you."

He moved his other hand, so it was drawing lazy circles over her softly rounded belly. Tori automatically sucked in her stomach, her entire body tensing beneath his touch. Moving a hand back, he gave her a quick swat on her bare ass, causing her to gasp.

"Don't you dare feel like you need to hide your curves from me. I felt you pull your muscles tight, and I won't have you thinking you aren't gorgeous just the way you are. Relax those muscles before you get another swat, sweetheart. I plan to memorize every dip and curve before the night is over." It took a couple of seconds, but she was finally able to relax into his touch.

"Such a good girl, thank you for that show of trust. Your body is incredible. I don't like women who are stick thin. I want a woman whose body is rounded and soft. I want to be able to squeeze you, to know it's a woman cuddled against me."

Good bumps raced over the surface of her skin at his sweet words, and she trembled again, but this time it wasn't from embarrassment.

"I want you to know how amazing you are. You're testing my control in ways I haven't experienced in so long, princess. Christ, you are undoing me."

Trace's words warmed her soul. Careful to keep her feet firmly planted, Tori sighed and leaned closer to him until there wasn't any space between his chest and her back.

"That's it, sweetheart, just relax into my touch. Let me

lead you right over the edge, princess. The angels certainly knew what they were doing when they sent you to me. Watching you lose yourself in your submission is such a turn-on."

His hands continued to caress sensual circles over her belly and lower abdomen but didn't touch her mound or her aching full breasts. He was purposely avoiding the areas where she most craved his touch to build up her pleasure, but he was also slowly driving her insane. Hell, the unhurried sweeps of his work-roughened hands over her silky softness were about to push her over the edge of desire.

"Jesus, Joseph, and Mary, you are making me pull every trick out of my bag of Dom secrets to stay control—and we're scraping the bottom, sweetness."

She wished he'd throw that damn bag away and fuck her already. *Geez, what's a girl have to do to get a little sex around here?*

TRACE HAD NEVER had a woman test his Dom instincts the way this one did. He'd topped Nan, but he'd never felt this burning desire to ravage and claim her. There was something about Victoria Paulson that drew him like a magnet to steel. He longed to feel her wet velvet walls clutching his sex and trying to pull him deeper. Tori's groan of pleasure brought him back to the moment.

"Tell me, my little snow angel, does that feel good?" When she didn't immediately respond with anything but a low groan, he stopped moving until he felt her body tense in awareness he'd asked her a question.

"Oh my God, it feels so good, I don't know how I'll stand anything more. My body feels like it's on fire, but I need... oh... God..." Tori was starting to quiver in his arms, and he tightened his grip on her because he knew the first touch to her engorged, aching clit was going to be enough to give her the release her body was craving.

With pinpoint accuracy, Trace moved his hands down to her mound, found her swollen clit, and gently pinched the little bundle of nerves peeking out from under its hood, seeking his touch. Tori screamed her release—her knees buckled, but Trace had been ready and easily kept her upright. He kept his hand between her legs and felt her juices flood his fingers. Using her body's natural lubrication, he plunged his middle finger into her pussy and felt her vaginal walls pulse and contract as she tumbled headlong into another orgasm, stronger than the first. He moved his finger in and out in short thrusts until he felt her coming back down from her release. Pulling his fingers free, he brought them to his mouth and licked them clean.

"Oh, princess, you taste wonderful. I can hardly wait to bury my face in your sweet pussy and lick you until you think you are going to lose your mind with need. Now that we have proven yet again you most assuredly are capable of having an orgasm, two in rapid succession, as a matter of fact, let's get you into another position, so I can get a little relief myself."

Trace moved her to the bedroom and smiled at her surprised expression when she took in the preparations he'd made in the enormous room. His bed was larger than king size and had been raised so when he'd bent Nan over the bed, she had been at the perfect level to accommodate his height. Thanking God for the years he'd had with Nan, he shook off the melancholy that usually followed a trip down memory lane and shifted his focus to the tiny woman standing in front of him. He'd carried her down the hall and set her on her feet just inside the room and waited patiently, giving her a moment to observe the mood he'd tried to create in the spacious suite.

He'd spent time earlier in the evening setting up the soft lighting and mirrors, and he was rewarded by Tori's expression the minute they'd entered the suite. It had been dark last night when he'd moved her to his bed, and she would have been in a hurry to get downstairs this morning, so he was sure she hadn't really taken the time to visually take in the room until this moment. Trace had never liked surprising subs by moving them into unfamiliar areas, then just fucking them. He'd always found their responses to be much more open and genuine if they were aware and comfortable with their surroundings.

"Take a couple of minutes to look around, Tori. I'm going to take a quick shower, and when I return, I expect you to be bent over the edge of the bed with your legs spread wide and your back arched, so the first thing I see when I exit the bath is your gorgeous ass and your sweet pussy all red and swollen from your release.

"Don't clean yourself up, I want to see your juices making your pretty pussy lips all wet and glistening with your cream coating the petals of your swollen sex." He saw her eyes flash with something that looked much too close to embarrassment, so he shook his head and continued.

"I saw that look, and don't you dare be ashamed of the juices I was so pleased to feel, smell, and taste. Your release was a gift you gave to me, and if I ask that you leave the evidence of that gift and present it to me again, I'll accept no less." With those words, he moved to the bath and left her standing there, looking stunned by his words.

When Tori finally realized Trace had gone, she remembered his instructions to look around and enjoyed the
opportunity to explore his bedroom. The room was
enormous with floor-to-ceiling windows along one side.
The French doors in the center of the wall appeared to lead
to a deck, and she moved closer, wondering what lay
beyond. Peering through the glass, she could see the deck
was large with twinkling lights, highlighting the edges and
steps leading down.

There was a hot tub off to one side she was sure would
easily accommodate ten people and a nice set of loungers
with a small table between them. The deck was sheltered
and even though she could see the snow swirling beyond
the deck, the wooden platform itself was clear. She could
imagine him entertaining a special guest and unwinding
outside while enjoying what was probably a gorgeous view
of his backyard and spectacular mountains beyond. The
tiny lights looked like fairies dancing on the snow drifting
at the edge of the deck, and she didn't even realize she was
still standing mesmerized by the sight until she felt Trace's
hands on her waist.

"Princess, this is not where you were supposed to be, but
I'm willing to give you a pass on this if you'll share your
thoughts with me." Trace had come out of the shower
faster than he would have normally because he couldn't

wait any longer to get inside Tori. Because he'd rushed, he hadn't been surprised she wasn't in position yet, but he had been surprised to find her gazing out at the back deck as if she'd become completely lost in the view.

He watched her reflection in the windows for several long seconds, and she'd seemed to be focused on the lights twinkling at the wood deck's edge. He'd put the lights along the edge as a safety measure, but had often found himself standing where Tori stood, lost in thought with his gaze focused in the exact same spot she seemed to be watching. Tori surprised him when she turned and looked up at him, her pupils dilated and her expression sincere.

"I'm sorry I wasn't where I was supposed to be. I just got so lost in thought looking out onto the deck, I guess I lost track of time. It's so lovely out there, and the lights look like tiny fairies dancing on top of the snow. I just kind of fell into that frame of thought and zoned out. I noticed the large hot tub and knew you must entertain um... well, umm, special friends out there in the summer. I could almost see you relaxing back on the chaise lounge afterward with a drink on the table. You'd be able to enjoy what I'm sure is an amazing view, no matter the season." She tucked her chin and dropped her gaze after her sincere reply, but not before he'd seen the longing in her eyes. There was something so special about this woman, he was amazed at how connected he felt to her despite having only met her a few hours earlier.

Lifting her chin so that her eyes met his, he spoke slowly. "Princess, you are one remarkable woman. Everything you said about the lights along the edge of the snow? I have had those exact same thoughts. The only thing you didn't get right was the part about the special guests being on that deck, in this bedroom, or in my home. I think this is a good time to tell you that I have not had any women, aside from the wives of friends or members of my family, in my home since my wife died, and none of those women have ever been in this room. This house had barely gotten off the architect's table when Nan died, so we never shared it as our home."

He could feel her relax into his arms. *Aha, so my little sub is a bit possessive. Good to know because I don't share either.* He enjoyed bringing in another Dom if he knew it was something his sub would enjoy, but any sharing was confined to rare scenes. Even though he had several friends who either had or were pursuing polyamorous relationships, he knew that would never be for him.

"Now, let's get you into position, I want to have a look at what you have entrusted to me."

Tori's breathing accelerated in anticipation, and he could smell her arousal. He could see the confusion in her eyes and wondered what internal debate she was waging. When she gave a weak half chuckle, he wasn't willing to let it go.

"Want to share what you find so funny, princess?" Trace knew Tori would be able to hear the note of irritation in his voice, and she immediately ducked her head, looking guilty for being disrespectful.

She turned to face him and said, "I'm sorry, I didn't intend to be hurtful. I swear I wasn't laughing at you. I was thinking about how ridiculous it is to feel embarrassed about you looking at my, well, um... my privates when you have already made me come twice. I'm pretty sure you have seen women naked before, so it won't really be any big deal for you."

Trace moved so fast, he doubted she'd even realized he had until she found herself laid over his lap. *What the heck happened and when did he sit on this chair? Holy shit, he moves fast.*

Trace gave two sharp swats to both ass cheeks and watched them quickly turn a delicious shade of pink.

"Stop making it seem as if you are not anything special. I've had enough of that, and I have warned you, but you don't seem to be figuring it out, so I'll try another approach." The next swats were right on top of the crease between her ass and upper thighs. She was going to feel those with every step she took for the rest of the evening, and that was exactly the reminder he'd been seeking.

Trace knew a lot of Doms who thought the harder the spanking, the more it taught a lesson, but he had never found that to be true. He liked to use well-placed, stinging swats that left a lingering tenderness long after the spanking was done as a reminder of the sub's error and the consequences they'd face if it was repeated.

"Now, I'm going to give you four more swats, and I want you to count them after each one, do you understand, Tori? I want to make it perfectly clear you are getting this punishment because you have continued trying to diminish your value to me, and I have simply listened to all of that bullshit I intend to."

Tori's voice was shaky, and he could tell she was crying. Trace knew she wasn't in great pain, her reaction was more likely because she felt bad for letting him down. She was clearly someone who liked to please others, and his displeasure with her was what was really causing her tears.

She carefully counted off the last four swats, and when they were over, he pulled her up onto his lap, so he could wipe her tears.

"Sweetness, you are an amazing woman, and I want you to understand how very special you are. I have helped train many subs, and I was married to a woman who tried to be a sub for many years before we both gave up on the idea. But you? Oh, princess, you are so very precious, and I can't stand it when you don't recognize the fact I am enchanted by you."

Tori looked up into his eyes, searching for any hint of sarcasm or teasing but didn't detect anything other than sincerity. Could he really see something in her no other man before him had seen? The two guys she'd dated in college never cared anything about making sure she felt valued. And her stalker in Houston had just wanted to own her... his desire to possess her had been all consuming.

Just thinking about Officer Gary George still had the power to make her almost physically ill. The sheer terror she'd lived under for so long had shaken her to her core and nearly destroyed her. She knew Trace had only given her the spanking to make her realize how many times she had devalued herself, and for some odd reason, it endeared him to her even more. The only thing troubling about the spanking was how hot it had made her, and she really didn't understand how that could be.

She remembered reading somewhere about how closely pleasure and pain were interpreted by the brain. At the time, she had discounted the information, assuming the words had obviously been written by a masochist, but now, she was going to have to rethink her uninformed observation. Before she could sort it through in her fractured thoughts, it occurred to her she might well have other misconceptions as well. Holy hell, how many other fallacies was she harboring about her own sexuality?

Trace used his calloused thumbs to brush aside her tears, and she realized he was watching her with such intensity, she wondered if he could read her mind as she tried to process all the feelings bombarding her. He hadn't spoken while she tried to sort out all the conflicting emotions, but she knew he was simply giving her time to wade through the emotional swamp on her own.

"Let me take a guess here and speculate that you are wondering why a spanking would turn you on so much, am I right, princess?"

She felt her eyes widen in surprise and he chuckled.

"Damn, I sure hope you don't play poker, sweetheart." When she tried to avert her gaze, Trace held her face to his, he wasn't going to let her hide from him as she spoke.

"Yes, it's so confusing. I don't understand it at all. It didn't really hurt so much as it stung, but the heat seemed to go to umm... well, to other parts of me... and in a big hurry, too."

Trace didn't even try to suppress his chuckle. "Well, sweetness, there are some really complicated answers to that question, but the short version is the body's interpretation of sexual pleasure and pain are very, very similar. The line between what your mind tells you are polar opposites is easily blurred. I see from your expression you aren't convinced, and that's okay for now. I'll explain more about that later, but right at this moment, I want to see exactly how that spanking affected you, so up you go. I want you to move over to the bed and get into position."

TORI HURRIED TO get her body positioned as Trace had instructed earlier. As he stood back and looked at her, he couldn't help but send up a prayer of thanks to God because she was fucking amazing. Tori Paulson was a goddess, her lushly rounded ass a beautiful red, the tops of her long legs forming a perfect frame for her pussy lips swollen with arousal. The folds of her labia were engorged with blood, telling him she was aroused, and they glistened beautifully with her slick honey. Knowing her body had prepared itself for his possession made him want to fuck her until they both collapsed in exhaustion.

From where he stood, Trace could just make out the soft round curves of her breasts and wondered how she would react to nipple clamps, or even better, nipple clamps attached to a clit clip, so each breath she took caused a pull on both ends of a jeweled chain. He was already designing it in his head and would talk to their local jeweler as soon as possible.

Climax was lucky enough to have a hometown crafts-man who was also a Dom, so he was always more than happy to craft specialty kink items on the side. He'd recently heard the man's kink line was selling like wildfire through his website. Trace made a mental note to check it out now that he had a woman to decorate.

Wow! When did I start thinking about Tori as my woman? Fuck! Who am I kidding? She was mine the minute I laid eyes on her outside the bar.

Running his hands up her thighs, he positioned his en-gorged cock at her entrance and pushed to the hilt without giving her a chance to tighten in resistance. Trace had wanted to give her the sweet burn of tissues forced to stretch suddenly to accommodate his size. He heard her gasp in surprise and was grateful she'd been drenched in desire and more than ready for him.

"Oh, sweetness you are so very wet for me. That makes me damned happy, not to mention extremely horny knowing your body was anxiously awaiting my possession." He took several steadying breaths before continuing, "Holy mother of all things sacred, the feel of your pussy rippling along my cock is so hot, it has to be just this side of heaven. I could happily stay right here the rest of my days."

Trace began to slowly withdraw from her depths, then set a random pace, keeping her on edge and ensuring she was continually trying to stretch back to get just a bit more. He wanted to keep her right on the cusp of release while he built her up further and further. He planned to give her an orgasm she would remember forever. He was going to hold off until she was so desperate, her mind fractured from pure pleasure even if his cock was already screaming for him to get on with it.

"Feel how the ridge around the head of my cock caresses the inside of your vagina? Can you feel my cock pulsing with a desperate need to release so hot, it feels like a raging wildfire? That's what you do to me, princess. You're tearing down every defense I've carefully held in place for years. Nothing exists at this moment but my raw and desperate need to be inside you. Grab on to the covers, princess because I'm going to fuck you hard, and I don't want you moving away from me."

As soon as he saw her delicate fingers grip the coverlet on top of the bed, he began a brutal, pounding pace, plunging into her sweet depths again and again until sweat beaded on his forehead and rolled down the sides of his face. With each stroke, he could feel his cock hitting her cervix. God, she felt amazing. When he felt the telltale flutters of her internal muscles, he pulled out and repositioned her, so her ass was just barely over the edge of the bed, and he could see her beautiful face.

Trace pulled her legs up, draping them over his arms as he canted his hips with a forceful jerk that shoved his cock back in all the way. He loved this position because he could easily tilt her until the rigid ring of his corona slid over the spongy spot inside. Trace would tease her G-spot until he was ready to send her straight into orbit.

He could also see her face, and he loved watching her breasts jiggle each time he bottomed out inside her. She was so small-framed, he could literally tilt her up enough he could see the movement of his cock from the outside as it moved in her lower abdomen. God, what a rush *that* was. Before he realized it, the moment was there, and he angled her hips perfectly and launched them both right over the edge into space.

TORI DIDN'T KNOW what happened. She hadn't realized it was coming until her body was already responding to something Trace had done deep inside her. Suddenly, all she could see was a million colors exploding in her vision. It was like being caught in a time warp where things moved at lightning speed, but it was playing out in slow motion. She wondered if she'd fallen into a vortex of some kind because she could have sworn she left her body for several seconds.

She heard a scream and wondered who the hell was screaming, but she couldn't form a coherent thought to ask… hell, if she was honest, she didn't really care either because, at that moment, nothing mattered but the pleasure. Something in the back of her mind told her she was the one making all the noise, but she pushed aside the embarrassment of that realization. Certain she'd heard Trace's shout of completion, she was grateful he'd found release as well, and it warmed her heart to know she had helped him get there.

Floating? How could she be floating? What did it matter? Yes, indeed, she was floating just above the bed, and it felt amazing. When she felt Trace pull out, she crashed back down onto the cool sheets, but she didn't even have enough energy to stir. He returned with a warm, damp washcloth to wipe away the stickiness between her thighs before blotting the area dry. There was a small place in the back of her mind that protested the action as too intimate, but she was so spent, she could only manage to groan as she tried in vain to close her legs.

"Hold on, princess, you'll sleep much better after I have cleaned you a bit. It is a Dom's privilege to care for his sub in *all* ways, and I want to make sure you rest comfortably." The soft tone of his voice, as well as the soothing reassurance of his words, soothed her, and she let the darkness wash over her and tumbled head first into a deep sleep.

Trace watched her sleep for a long while, entranced at how she calmed with his words and touch. *She was made just for me. She is amazing. Mine!* He was no longer surprised by his connection to her and wondered how he had gotten lucky enough to find two women during his lifetime who were so perfect for him.

He and Nan had been college sweethearts, and he'd loved her more than life itself. He'd been disappointed she'd had never been able to embrace his lifestyle, but their sex life had been enough, and he wouldn't trade their time together for anything in the world. But it was easy to see Tori was his other half, her sexual needs meshed perfectly with his own, and for long moments, he considered how he was going to keep her safe.

Trace wasn't a fool; if her stalker was determined to find her, he would, and something told him the bastard who'd made her life a living hell wouldn't give up easily. Deciding to check in with Dylan and Alex about the progress they'd made, he moved the covers, so Tori would be warm while he stepped from the room to make the calls.

Chapter 8

C ORT DOUGLAS COULDN'T remember a time when his emotions had swung so far, one extreme to the other. Holding Sally in his arms after she'd been brutally abused by a Dom at ShadowDance was a study in sharp contrasts, that was for damned sure.

On one end, he was outraged at the way she'd been treated and couldn't wait for her to settle down enough he could find out exactly how she'd found herself in such a dangerous predicament. But on the other hand, holding her tiny form against his chest, feeling her soft breath wash over his neck like a warm summer breeze was as close to heaven as he'd experienced in years.

People assumed because he trained the subs at The ShadowDance Club that he used his position for unlimited sex, but that had never been the case. He'd been a member of the Lamonts' club for several years and had been the trainer for almost that entire time, and not once had he had sex at ShadowDance or with a submissive he was training.

Hell, once he'd laid eyes on Sally, he'd lost all interest in other women. She was everything he'd never known he wanted. She worked as the head of the Housekeeping Department at the club, and he'd never known anyone who worked harder. Sally was well liked by everyone who knew her, and the staff who worked under her supervision raved about her.

Alex and Zach had marveled at how quickly she had transformed a department that had given them nothing but trouble into the one area they never spent any time double-checking. With Alex and Zach's help, she'd help set up onsite child care for her co-workers, and the absenteeism rate had fallen to virtually nothing. Cort knew she was living in a small guest cottage at the back of the ranch, and he often saw her outside playing with her young daughter.

When he felt her begin to settle, Cort shifted, so he could speak to her face-to-face.

"Sally, we need to discuss what happened here tonight. Are you up to helping me understand how this came about?" Cort knew he'd have to tread carefully because of his personal interest in the woman looking at him from beneath tear-dampened lashes. He certainly didn't want to make her feel ashamed of her actions or fearful of his response. When she silently nodded her assent, he continued. "All right, thank you for agreeing to help me piece this together. Now, during his ravings to Alex and Zach, Master Jacobs mentioned you'd turned him down before. What made you agree to a scene with him tonight?"

Sally took several deep breaths before she looked directly into his eyes and answered in a shaky voice. "He told me you ordered it, that because I hadn't agreed to be with him before, he had taken his complaint to you, and as the trainer for The Club's submissives, you'd instructed him to tell me I was to allow it as a punishment for being so picky." Cort stared at her in shock, completely and utterly speechless. He could only sit in stunned silence and watch helplessly as tears ran down her cheeks in steady rivulets.

When he didn't respond immediately, she continued, "I didn't want you to be disappointed in me, so I agreed even though I was so scared of him, I could hardly breathe. I love ShadowDance, and I didn't want to do anything that might threaten my good standing here."

The sorrow he saw in her eyes nearly broke his heart, and for a few heart-wrenching seconds, all he could do was pull her into his tight embrace and try to get his emotions settled. The last thing she needed was the raging out-of-control response that kept threatening to erupt. Several minutes later, he'd finally regained enough control to speak in what he hoped was his normal Dom/Trainer voice.

"Never, ever would I make such a decision because, first and foremost, it's not my decision to make. He did not speak to me about you or your refusal to scene with him, and if he had, I would have come to you immediately to hear your side. I want you to know that *you*... and *only you* make the decisions about what happens to you at ShadowDance. Safe, sane, and consensual are not trite words we give lip service to, Sally. They are the guiding tenants of everything that occurs in this club. Those words are in place to protect you, sweetness."

He pulled her against his chest again and tried to slow his breathing, so she didn't pick up on the pure white-hot rage coursing through his blood. He swore if the man wasn't out of the club by the time he got to Alex and Zach's office, he'd take his sorry ass apart, piece by piece. How dare he lie to Sally and use him as a reason to hurt her? Cort was literally seeing red before he was able to get himself calmed down. Pulling out his cell phone from the clip on his belt, he speed dialed Zach and quickly relayed the details Sally had provided. It was important they made certain she didn't have to face the jackass who'd brutalized her.

After he'd relayed all the details to Zach, the other man

reminded him they'd asked him to take the rest of the night off and attend to Sally. Zach told him they'd reserved a private room, and it had already been fully stocked with everything they felt he might need for her aftercare.

"Sweetness, did you hear what Master Zach had to say?" Knowing she had likely heard Zach's deep baritone voice through the hand-held device, he wasn't surprised at her quick nod. He ran his thumb over her lower lip in a gentle caress and looked deeply into her eyes before he went on. "I want you, Sally. Not as a trainee but as a submissive woman. I want you to know if you agree to go to that room with me tonight, it won't be only for aftercare. Do you understand?" When she nodded slowly, he said, "Sally, that isn't good enough. I need to hear you say the words."

"Yes, Sir, I understand. I want you, too. I have wanted you for a long time." Her voice was quiet, but there was no hesitancy in it, and Cort was on his feet before she'd even finished her answer. He cradled her against his chest and was striding down the hall to the private room Zach had directed him to with the determined look and motions of a man intent on staking a long-overdue claim. He felt Sally bury her face against his neck, breathing in his scent, and heard her sigh in contentment and wondered how everything could have seemed so terribly wrong a half hour ago and now, things felt so very right.

As soon as he made his way into the Queen Anne private room, he set Sally on her feet and kissed her. Cort's plan to take his time and savor her sweet body was nearly short-circuited by the blistering kiss they shared. When he felt her body melt against his, he considered just making love her for the rest of the night but knowing how perfectly she responded to being dominated was just too sweet to resist.

Breaking their kiss, Colt stepped back and crossed his arms over his chest, giving Sally his best Dom expression.

"I want to remind you, my sweet sub, if we continue, you are *mine*. Are you prepared for everything that means?"

Cort watched as Sally's eyes dilated until there was little more than a small ring of color surrounding pupils opened wide by desire. When she slowly nodded her head and quietly said, "Yes, Sir," he let out the breath he hadn't even known he was holding.

"Very good, my sweet. Have you ever used the Fucking Throne, Sally?" He heard her breath hitch, watched the base of her neck, and saw her pulse kick up. *Aha, I'd say you are turned on by the idea even though I already know the answer to my question. You are in for a real treat, sweet subbie.* As she answered, he was slowly leading her toward the large chair in the corner. The ornate piece was designed to remind the casual observer of a typical Queen Anne chair, but this one had a few interesting "modifications" that made it a real treat for a sub.

Cort watched Sally closely as he began securing her to the chair. He casually explained how the chair worked and was pleased to see how her breathing shifted. Soon her breaths were so shallow and fast, she was nearly panting, and he hadn't even finished strapping her in yet.

Once she was secured and could no longer see what was happening behind her, he moved into place and slid aside the hidden seat panel which bared her pussy to his touch. Finding her more than ready, he quickly sheathed a dildo and slid it into place, securing it with the Velcro straps attached to the bottom of the chair. Picking up the remote control from the armoire, he stepped in front of

Sally and slowly loosened his leathers until his painfully hard cock was bobbing in front of her. He smiled when she licked her lips.

"Like what you see, little subbie?" Cort nearly laughed out loud when her eyes never left his cock as she nodded her head. "Sally, I asked you a question. Let's not start our time together with me being forced to paddle your sweet ass."

"Y-yes, Sir. I like what I see."

Cort loved the breathy way she'd answered his question. Next time, he'd make her actually look at his eyes when she responded, but he was enjoying her perusal too much right now to make an issue of it.

With Sally's focus centered on his cock, he was able to start the small motor that rotated the dildo in her dripping passage without her having a chance to tense up. When she gasped, he didn't try to hide his amusement. He stepped forward onto the small foot pads on either side of the chair bringing his cock directly in front of her sweet lips.

"Okay, sweet girl, you know what to do. But I'm warning you now, I have been waiting so long to feel your luscious lips wrapped around my aching cock, I may not last long." He laughed softly when he saw her straining against the straps holding her tightly to the chair, her pink tongue flicking out, just reaching the outer ridge of his engorged cock head.

Cort knew Sally had to feel like he was spinning her closer and closer to the epicenter of a huge storm because she was clearly edging toward sub-space. He'd no sooner gotten the words, "Open up, baby" and pushed his raging cock against her lips than she felt the machine speed up. As soon as she tightened her lips around him and sucked him to the back of her throat, he knew it was time to exercise a bit of control, so Cort slowed the machine.

"I know what you're trying to do, you know? I won't let you top from the bottom. You know better than that, my sweet little sub. Now, unless you want me to light up that beautiful ass of yours, you'll play by the rules. If you come before I give you permission, I'll move the machine back a few inches and change out the dildo, so it's not nearly as pleasant an experience for you."

Cort almost laughed out loud at her instant response. She refocused her attention to giving him a mind-bending blow job, and when he sped up, then tilted the angle of the machine fucking her sweet pussy, he could smell her arousal. When she groaned around him, he knew he was too far gone. Sliding the control to the fastest setting, he managed to bark out the command.

"Come for me!"

The words had to have still been bouncing around the room when Cort saw Sally stiffen, and when she screamed her release, he felt as if someone had detonated an electrical charge in his balls. His cum pulsed in long streams down Sally's welcoming throat.

When he finally felt stable enough to stand without clutching the chair behind Sally's head, he moved back, knelt in front of her, and kissed her, hoping his lips could convey the emotions his voice wasn't recovered enough to say. Thank heaven, he'd remembered to hit the "kill" switch right away, so he didn't need to worry she was still being penetrated when they were both gasping for air, trying to recover.

When he was finally able to walk, he quickly unfastened her from the chair and carried her to the bed. Cuddling her close, he kissed the tip of her nose and each of her eyes as she closed them, letting sleep pull her under.

Even though he knew she had fallen asleep, he whispered, "You are mine, you know. I've wasted enough time, and even if your heart isn't there yet, your body already recognizes its Master." Pulling her tighter into his embrace, he slid into a contented sleep, holding the woman who had just claimed him, heart and soul.

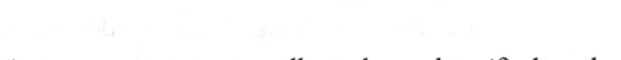

TRACE MADE SEVERAL calls and was horrified at the results of the background check his friends had run on Gary George. The information on case reports relating to Victoria Paulson were even worse. Tori had made dozens of police reports concerning stalking and violence but had received little more than lip service responses and often, not even that much.

Her dog had been killed, her car damaged several times and ultimately destroyed, her home burglarized, and all her belongings destroyed more than once. She'd changed her mobile phone number several times and finally, just abandoned it in favor of throwaway models that were basically only good for placing emergency calls. She had finally been asked to resign from her position at the law firm because Officer George had harassed her coworkers to the point none of them felt safe. But perhaps worst of all, the sweet woman sleeping so peacefully in his bed had lost all but one of her friends because they'd been too afraid to be near her, fearing they or their families would also be targeted. The injustice of it was almost more than Trace would comprehend.

Mitch Grayson, the computer guru for ShadowDance, had easily accessed Tori's medical records as well as all the police reports despite the fact they'd been buried deep. Doctor's records indicated she'd shown signs of extreme stress, and two different physicians had noted she was a prime candidate for PTSD. Mitch was a former Special Forces soldier and had given Trace a brief rundown of symptoms to watch for and suggestions for ways to alleviate the stress the symptoms might already be causing her.

After Alex, Zach, and Dylan had disconnected from the conference call, Mitch had asked him directly, "Are you interested in her, Trace? If you are, I'm going to secure most of this information because I want it to be for your eyes only. There is a lot I didn't mention in the call with everyone else because I wanted to talk with you first."

Trace wasn't surprised by Mitch's observation, the man was an empath and often heard the thoughts of other people, but still, his consideration was welcome. Trace explained his instant connection to Tori and asked Mitch to follow through suppressing the information and asked that he also give a heads-up to his wife, Rissa, that he'd be bringing Tori around to dinner and would appreciate if she and the other women would make Tori feel as welcome as possible. Mitch assured him Rissa would be happy to help. He also promised to speak with Katarina and Jenna. Both women would be happy to focus on welcoming Tori to their makeshift family.

After ending the call, Trace poured himself a small glass of scotch and sat watching the last flames flicker in the fireplace. He was lost in thought about how to best help Tori when her scream pierced the silence. He was sprinting down the hall when he heard what sounded like someone falling to the floor. As he entered the room, he nearly panicked when he didn't see Tori on the bed.

He'd left the bedside lamp on, so she wouldn't wake up in a dark room, and in its soft glow, he caught movement in the corner of the room. Moving to squat in front of her cowering form, he reached out to her, and she screamed and tried to bat his hands away.

"No! No! Please! I'm begging you, don't touch me! I can't believe you killed her! Why? Why?" She started to cover her face, only to curl further into a ball, wrapping her arms covering her head as if protecting herself from an unseen attacker.

Trace moved back a foot or so and spoke to her in soft tones. "Tori, wake up, Princess, it's me, Trace. You're safe now, please wake up. Come back to me, sweetheart." Her gasping breaths and sobbing were tearing him apart. "Come on, Tori, wake up and look at me." He used his Dom voice and was grateful when he heard the quick hitch in her breathing.

Tori slowly moved her arms away from her head and looked up with wide-eyed fear, and Trace swore he wanted nothing more than to make sure that look of terror never filled her beautiful dark eyes again.

"That's it, Princess, look at my face. It's Trace, and you are safe with me. When you know who I am, reach out for my hand. I don't want to frighten you further by reaching for you." This was one of the things Mitch had just told him to use when dealing with a PTSD victim, and he would make a point to thank his friend for his insight and guidance because the shift in her body language was almost immediate after he'd spoken the words to her.

Slowly, he could see her focus return, and she lifted her hand to him at almost the same time she launched her delicate body into his arms. Her deep sobs were gut-wrenching, but Trace held her as they sat together on the floor. He let her vent all the pent-up emotion as he rocked her.

"It's okay, Princess, let it out. You're safe now, but I want you to purge yourself of all that fear and sadness. I'll hold you for as long as it takes." Trace was sure his heart cracked nearly in two as he held her close while the storm raged within her. He couldn't imagine what horrors she'd been through, and he was sure having to do so without any support from friends or family would have been more than most people would have been able to survive.

Trace could feel her desolation and understood why Tori would feel completely flattened by the nightmare, so he kept his words soothing as he held her. The torrent of several months pent up emotions bubbled to the surface, and he kept his arms wrapped securely around her because, honest to God, he was sure she was going to fly apart. When she was finally able to speak again, she kept her face against his broad chest.

"I'm so sorry, I have nightmares sometimes, but I don't usually completely lose it like this."

"Shhh, Princess, I'm so sorry your life has been so de-railed by a lunatic. You didn't deserve that treatment, hell, no woman does. But I'm very grateful for your trust in me, and I'm going to do everything in my power to keep you safe from harm." He was rubbing his hand in slow circles over her trembling back and noticed how small she felt in his arms.

"I'm curious, Tori, I love your curves, but I have the feeling you've lost weight and muscle tone as a result of this stress. Did you have to give up your workouts when all of this started, princess?" His gut feeling was confirmed by her nod. "Well, we'll see what we can do about getting you back up to your previous fitness level, what do you say?

You'll feel much more in control of things when you're physically strong again." He chuckled, trying to lighten the mood a bit and was pleased when she tilted her tear-streaked face up and gave him a small grin.

"I'm not too sure I want to gain any weight because it's always been hard for me to stay slender, but I like the idea of being able to defend myself. I tried to take a class, but they asked me to not attend anymore when he kept harassing the staff for trying to help me." Tori sighed, and Trace was completely taken in by her defeated expression.

"Well, I have some friends who will love teaching you all types of self-defense. There are several Doms at ShadowDance who are former Special Forces soldiers, and any of them will be happy to help." Grinning ear to ear, he went on, "But Jenna Lamont, soon to be Jenna Lamont-Matthews, kicks the asses of most of them any time she can sucker them into sparring with her. I know she'd be more than happy to help in any way she can although you may have to wait until after her wedding on Christmas Eve."

Trace was pleased by the smile he saw light Tori's face at his suggestions. He pulled his phone from his pocket and sent a quick text to several of his friends, explaining Tori's need, and despite the late hour, he received affirmative responses from eight different people, including Jenna, within minutes. When he showed her the responses, he saw tears fill her eyes again but knew they were tears of gratitude, not sadness.

"Princess, I want you to know that no one in Climax will walk away from you because they are afraid of your stalker. You're going to see very quickly how we do things in our small town. You'll have a wall of friends the bastard will have to get through to even look at you. These are good people, wonderful friends who will look this challenge right in the eye. Hell, they won't even blink." Trace watched her, knowing she was trying to wrap her mind around the fact she was no longer being left alone to face the dangers she'd been buried under for so long.

"Do you really think they'll help me? I mean, they don't even know me, and well, I don't want to put anyone else in danger." Tori's focus on protecting others was enough to make him fall further in love with her. He was startled by the direction his thoughts were taking and wondered again how his heart was easily moving at such a breakneck pace. He patiently explained why Jenna had responded so quickly and the other woman's reason for insisting she be allowed to help. Hearing Jenna had learned self-defense as the result of an attack years ago filled Tori's expression with compassion. He didn't fill her in on all the details because he felt it wasn't his story to tell, and Tori seemed to understand that perfectly.

"We're going to dinner at ShadowDance very soon, so you'll have a chance to meet everyone then. But for now, let's get you back into bed and settled. I'm afraid this floor is awfully hard, and my ass is getting cold." Laughing, he helped her stand, then accepted her hand as she helped him to his feet as well.

He smiled at her kindness and pulled her into his embrace before releasing her to use the restroom while he straightened the bed. When she returned, he wrapped her in his arms, spooning her from behind, loving how perfectly she fit against him, her perfect ass nestled against his rapidly growing cock. He smiled to himself and tried to recite baseball statistics in order to distract his libido.

Trace was pleased when he heard Tori's breathing level out as she fell back to sleep. Breathing in the sweet scent of her shampoo and her own unique fragrance, he closed his eyes and fell into a contented sleep.

Chapter 9

New Year's Eve

ORI STOOD IN the doorway of The ShadowDance Club and looked around as Trace greeted everyone, calling each person by name. She loved the feeling of belonging she was finally starting to recognize, but she was still struggling to fully accept it as her new reality, trust just wasn't easy for her. Trace had warned her the club would be particularly crowded tonight, and he'd been right. They'd attended several times before, and she hadn't seen this many people during all of her previous visits put together. The main lounge alone held more people than she'd seen in the entire town. Where had all these people come from?

Trace still hadn't asked her to do anything in public, and she was grateful for that. She sensed a particular unease in him tonight, and she found herself worrying he was tiring of her already. They'd fallen into an easy routine. She was working with the elderly local attorney to learn his practice while her license was being transferred to Colorado. She'd taken the small test required and hadn't had any problems thanks to Mr. Sherman's tutoring sessions. Tori smiled, thinking about her elderly, legal mentor who was nearly ninety years old and still a ball of energy. She adored his witty wisdom, and they had become fast friends.

Mrs. Sherman was the light of his life, and after Tori had met her, it was obvious the feeling was mutual. As she'd watched them together, Tori wondered what it would be like to have a spouse who loved you unconditionally. How wonderful would it be to be married to someone who thought the sun rose and set in you and didn't make any attempt to hide their affection when in public? Sighing to herself, the noises of the club were a stark reminder she needed to pay attention to what was happening around her, so she didn't inadvertently offend someone with her inattention.

Trace had rarely let her out of his reach any other time they'd been at the club, but tonight, he seemed almost distracted, and she found herself standing alone against a wall toward the back of the club's main lounge. Looking over the sea of faces, she kept reminding herself to refrain from making direct eye contact with the other Doms, something the lawyer in her struggled with each time they'd been here. Eye contact was such a huge part of her professional life, she always worried about offending one of the stricter Doms. The other subs had warned her about several of the Doms, and she did her best to steer clear of them. The thought of any man other than Trace punishing her sent shards of icy fear racing through her each time she even entertained the thought.

Thinking back over the numerous dinners she'd had at the Lamonts' home, she shuddered when she remembered how Trace hadn't let her wear underwear and how she'd quickly figured out why as he'd brought her to orgasm right at the table... during dinner, for God's sake. She'd been mortified until she realized each of the women he'd introduced her to that first night had suffered a similar fate. The other women had welcomed her, but she had spent the most time with Kat and Jenna. Kat had invited her for tea on a couple of occasions and had been a great source of information about the procedures related to The Shadow-Dance Club.

Tori had laughed at the small woman until she'd cried when she couldn't get out of the chair and had pleaded with Tori to help, then begged her to not tell her husbands about the incident. Kat had said Alex and Zach were already hovering over her to the point she was about to "go postal," and if they heard she couldn't get out of a chair without help, she'd never get out of their sight. Tori had crossed her heart in a great dramatic fashion and sworn she'd take the secret to her grave. She wished Kat was here tonight but knew her new friend would be in her suite with her feet propped high if her husbands had any say about it. And after meeting Alex Lamont, she was certain he had plenty to say.

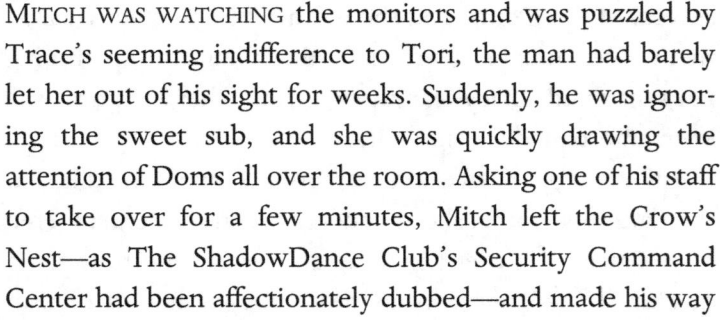

MITCH WAS WATCHING the monitors and was puzzled by Trace's seeming indifference to Tori, the man had barely let her out of his sight for weeks. Suddenly, he was ignoring the sweet sub, and she was quickly drawing the attention of Doms all over the room. Asking one of his staff to take over for a few minutes, Mitch left the Crow's Nest—as The ShadowDance Club's Security Command Center had been affectionately dubbed—and made his way down to the main lounge.

When he moved alongside Tori, she jumped when he

greeted her.

"Oh my gosh, Mitch, you startled me... oh damn, I mean Master Mitch... I'm sorry, I really am not very focused tonight." As her emotions flooded him, he knew she was struggling not to feel abandoned and was fighting the overwhelming fear she had worn out her welcome in Trace's life on top of her concern she was now messing up the rules in a big way.

Mitch placed his hand on her shoulder and turned her to face him.

"Tori, where is Trace? I saw him come in with you, but I didn't see where he got off to." He kept his touch neutral but was using it to help him pick up on her thoughts, and he was concerned about what he was hearing. Her body language was screaming her insecurity, and the hesitance he saw in her dark eyes reminded him of how she had looked the first time they'd met.

"I'm sorry, I don't know where he has gone... um, Sir. He just seemed to walk away as we entered this room." She had cast her eyes down, and Mitch felt the waves of anxiety working their way through her. He'd been watching her inch her way toward the back exit on the monitors and remembered how close he and Bryant Davis had come to losing their new wife, Rissa when she'd been attacked after ducking out that same door.

"Stay right where you are, Tori. It's not safe for you to step outside that door alone. I'll find Trace and be right back." He was satisfied she would wait for him to return when she nodded. He moved to the bar, intending to ask Cort Douglas if he'd spoken with Trace, but saw the bar was swamped, so he pulled his cell phone from his pocket, moved to a hallway, and dialed Trace's number.

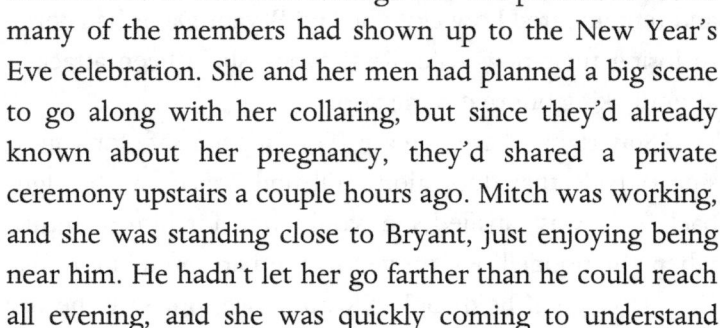

TORI SUDDENLY FELT like she was going to throw up, and she wasn't sure why. The man who had bumped into her had murmured an apology and even though she hadn't gotten a good look at him, there had been something oddly familiar about him, and she had the strangest feeling he'd bumped into her intentionally. *Did he poke me with a pin?* The question floated through her mind, but she brushed the question aside when he quickly moved on.

Within a few seconds, she was swaying on her feet. Dizziness swamped her, and her stomach began rolling as if she'd been dropped on the deck of a storm-tossed ship. Tori leaned against the wall, trying desperately to get her bearings. Looking across the room, she made eye contact with Rissa just before everything went black.

RISSA STOOD IN the Main Lounge and was pleased to see so many of the members had shown up to the New Year's Eve celebration. She and her men had planned a big scene to go along with her collaring, but since they'd already known about her pregnancy, they'd shared a private ceremony upstairs a couple hours ago. Mitch was working, and she was standing close to Bryant, just enjoying being near him. He hadn't let her go farther than he could reach all evening, and she was quickly coming to understand Kat's frustration with her husbands' overprotective natures.

Rissa had been happy to see Trace Bartell had brought the gorgeous young woman with long chestnut hair she had heard so much about and had spoken to briefly one evening at dinner. Rissa remembered the woman's name was Tori Paulson, but she hadn't really gotten a chance to get to know her. Suddenly, Rissa's eyes met those of Trace's date, and she was struck by the haunted look in the other woman's expression. Rissa smiled at her, remembering when she was the "new kid" and vowed to reach out to the woman whose shadowed expression reminded her so much of herself. There was something in Tori's expression that didn't look quite right to Rissa all of a sudden, and just as that thought made its way through her mind, Rissa watched as Tori's eyes seemed to roll up, then she disappeared from view.

Rissa screamed and took off running across the room with Bryant in hot pursuit. It was just seconds before they made it to the spot where she'd seen Tori disappear, and Rissa was in a panic when she couldn't find the other woman anywhere. Bryant turned Rissa to him, his eyes wild with concern.

"Love, what on earth is this about? What are you looking for? My God, you scared ten years off my life."

"She was right here… I saw her eyes roll back, then she just disappeared from view… she has to be here. Something bad has happened. Lock the doors. Do something! Oh my God!" Rissa was almost hysterical as she remembered everything that had happened to her so recently. She grabbed Bryant's shoulders and shook him. *"Please!* You have to do something, she is in danger, I can feel it!"

"Clarissa! *Stop!"* Alex Lamont stepped up beside Bryant, and the tone of his voice alone was enough to freeze Rissa in place. "Who are you talking about?" Alex demanded. As one of the owners of The ShadowDance Club, Alex was able to command attention just by his presence, but it was his power-filled aura as a Master that had Rissa spilling her story immediately.

"Tori Paulson. I saw her, I met her gaze, and something seemed off... like she wasn't well or something, then her eyes rolled up, and she just dropped from my view!" By the time Rissa had gotten it all out, Alex was already on his phone and men were pushing through the back door. Rissa could hear the newly installed outside alarms blaring just as the cold outside air blasted by her, causing her to shiver. Honestly, she wasn't sure it was only the frigid air that had chilled her to the bone, but her deep fear for the other woman's safety that was sending a steady stream of chills up and down her spine.

Bryant grabbed her hand, led her quickly to Alex and Zach's office, and sat her on the leather sofa. Just as he was turning to speak to her, Colt Matthews rushed in and seated his new bride, Jenna, next to Rissa. Colt looked at them both and warned, "Either of you moves from this room without one of us and you'll get such a paddling, you won't be able to sit for a week, understood?" When they both nodded, the men sprinted from the room.

"Holy shit, I've never seen Mr. Charming ever be so... well, Dom-like." Rissa saw Jenna shudder, head to toe, then a grin spread across her face just as a blush colored her cheeks a nice deep rose. "Well, I'm guessing that tone is reserved for playtime, ordinarily, am I right?" Now Rissa was practically laughing out loud at the look on Jenna's face. "Oh, for God's sake, woman, we are both newlyweds, and I'm pretty sure I'm not going to be shocked by anything you could tell me. Remember, I've worked with the members of this club for a while, and they've shared some pretty amazing stories with me."

"Okay, okay enough of that. Now fill me in, what the hell happened out there?" Jenna told Rissa that she had been standing next to Colt, lost in thought about starting classes in a couple weeks, their impending move into the addition being built onto the ShadowDance mansion, and the hundred and fifty-three things she needed to get started on when Colt answered his cell, then all but dragged her upstairs to her brothers' office before she'd even had time to blink. "He parked me here next to you, barked at us to stay put and was gone before I even asked a single question."

As Rissa told Jenna what had happened, they both moved to the windows and watched as the entire mountain seemed to have come alive. After the trouble a couple months ago, the lighting and security systems had been enhanced to the point the name ShadowDance was something of a joke. If all the lighting was activated, the mountain was so brightly lit, it would have been seen as a glow for miles around, and there wasn't a chance in hell of a shadow surviving.

"Damn, those brothers of mine really are the masters of overkill, aren't they? This damn mountain can probably be seen from space. God help their children because they'll probably wrap the poor kids in Bubble Wrap for their first, oh I don't know, forty years or so!"

Rissa laughed with her friend and agreed their actions were completely over the top most of the time, but right now, she was awfully glad for their efforts. Wringing her hands, she turned to Jenna.

"Do you think she's all right? I mean, where on earth could she have gone? One minute she was right there, then she was just *gone!*"

"Oh shit, Rissa, I'm so sorry, I was so insensitive. They'll find her, you'll see. Cripes, girlfriend, no one is getting off this mountain without getting a fucking sunburn from all those lights. Hell, remember that Chevy Chase movie where he puts all those Christmas lights on his house and it blinds their neighbors? Just imagine trying to walk around out there without sunglasses." Rissa smiled at Jenna and was grateful for her kind words. Jenna's grin turned mischievous.

"Now, let's call Kat and give her the scoop. You know they have her under house arrest, too. We might as well settle in and make the best of our lockdown!"

KAT HAD BEEN thrilled her friends had called to fill her in on the excitement at the club, but she was worried sick for the sweet woman she'd talked with a few times when she'd had her over for tea. Trace had brought her to dinner too, but the chaos that was a ShadowDance meal wasn't exactly conducive to chit-chat. Kat had sat with Tori and chatted about how she'd come to return to Climax and listened as Tori shared the horrors of being stalked by a police officer in Houston.

Friendships forged through a shared history of being a victim seemed to be fast and strong ties, and Kat noticed those connections usually ran soul deep. When she finally came back from her little emotional side trip, Kat had asked rhetorically, "God, what is wrong with people these days?" She sighed and continued, "I swear some men just don't fucking get it... hey, do you hear that? Is that a siren? Look out the windows... my insane husbands installed those damned sliding, bulletproof doors over my windows, and the minute somebody farts in the wrong direction, those things slide closed over my windows, every door in this mansion locks electronically, and I'm a prisoner in thirty seconds flat."

Jenna and Rissa smiled at each other as they moved to the windows and watched as the Climax County EMS pulled to a stop in front of the club. They watched as Trace ran toward the ambulance carrying Tori in his arms. She looked like a rag doll, and it took Rissa's breath away. She had to back up and sit down before she dropped. Jenna disconnected the call, and just as she noticed Rissa lowering her head to between her knees, Colt, Mitch, and Bryant stormed into the room.

Chapter 10

TRACE HAD BEEN in the back hallway explaining to a very irate Mitch Grayson he hadn't been ignoring Tori but had, in fact, been meeting with a fellow Dom who also happened to be a jeweler. His friend had designed the most amazing engagement ring Trace had ever laid eyes on, and he had been planning to propose to Tori at the stroke of midnight. He admitted he'd been so nervous, he hadn't even noticed her tension, and his heart had nearly broken in two when Mitch had explained how Tori had interpreted his actions. They had just turned to make their way back to where Mitch had left her when they'd heard Rissa's scream, and all hell had broken loose.

Both men had heard Rissa's explanation to Alex and had hit the back door at a full run. They had been able to easily track whoever had taken Tori by his tracks in the freshly fallen snow, and the minute the security staff had hit the lights, the kidnapper had wisely dropped his precious cargo and made a run for it. Trace stopped to tend to Tori while Mitch had continued to pursue the man who had left her lying, nearly naked, in the damned snow. Mitch had cornered the man, and Dylan Marshall, the local sheriff had taken him into custody.

When Mitch made his way back to the club where Trace held Tori waiting for the ambulance, he'd told Trace it was likely the kid they had in custody was a patsy and wouldn't even know who he was working for. Trace didn't think there was any doubt who the young man was working for but proving it would be another matter.

TORI'S HEART AND respiration rates were awfully slow, but both had remained steady—and that was the only thing keeping Trace from falling over the edge into full-blown panic. He just kept thinking about how close he'd come to losing her. He'd already lost one woman he'd loved deeply, and he wasn't sure his soul would be able to survive another walk down that dark path.

When they'd heard the ambulance coming up the drive, Trace had run out to meet them, knowing full well she'd been drugged, and a few seconds could make all the difference in the world... how many times had he replayed the argument he and Nan had the night she'd stormed from the house for the last time? If he'd just talked to her for a few more seconds, she wouldn't have been T-boned at the intersection of the main highway... or if he hadn't held her arm for those last few seconds, begging her to reconsider her plans to leave, she would still be alive today.

Shaking his head in a futile attempt to push those pointless thoughts out of his head, he walked into the emergency room at the local hospital right behind the EMTs and followed them into the examination room despite the vehement protests of the nursing staff.

Doc Woods was just a few steps behind him and assured the nurse Trace had valuable information relevant to the patient's care, so the nurse he'd decided was possessed by the devil himself, finally backed off. Trace had a lot of respect for the elderly doctor. Hell, he'd known the man his entire life. Trace couldn't help but smile when Doc looked at him and simply said, "Talk to me" as he set about examining Tori.

Trace filled him in on everything that had happened, including her past experiences at the hands of a stalker before she'd moved to Colorado. Considering Climax was a very small community where the grapevine conveys information faster than the Internet, Trace figured it was likely Doc already knew who she was, where she'd been living, and all about her taking over old man Sherman's law practice.

Doc finally paused his examination. "Any idea what she was drugged with?" When Trace shook his head, the elderly man yelled down the hall, asking what the hell was taking the lab staff so long. If Trace hadn't been so worried about the beautiful woman lying too quietly in front of him, he might have been amused at Doc's gruff bedside manner; as it was, he was simply terrified of losing his precious snow angel.

TRACE PACED THE crowded waiting room, trying to tune out the cacophony of sounds surrounding him. He'd been run out of Tori's room while the nurses got her settled in the small hospital's Critical Care Unit. Since it would be a couple hours before the lab results were in, Doc had said he wanted to "Err on the side of the Angels" and keep her under careful watch until they knew exactly what she'd been injected with.

How the hell could it take so damned long to put one tiny woman in a bed? He was battling the urge to storm back down the hall when Doc strode into the room. Walking directly up to Trace, he spoke loud enough for everyone to hear but kept focused on Trace as he spoke.

"We'll have the tests back in an hour or so, but truthfully, I'm fairly certain it isn't anything we need to worry about. All her vitals are strong, and from what you have told me, it's more likely this was just meant to make her easier to take. If that's true, I doubt the intent would have been to harm her." He patted Trace on the forearm and continued, "We'll take good care of her. I promise you, I'm not losing another one of your women, Trace. Damn, it broke my heart we didn't get Nan in here in time..." The sadness was so evident on the elderly man's face, Trace's heart went out to him.

Rissa stepped up and gave Doc a long hug. The two of them had a lot of history between them, most of which Rissa had just recently learned. Finding out the man she'd always known as her grandmother's best friend was, in fact, her grandfather had been a tremendous shock. Trace knew they had just recently sat down and worked it all out between them.

"Doc, everyone knows how dedicated you are. Don't you be blaming yourself for things you can't control." The old man smiled at Rissa and pulled her close for another hug, his deep sigh showing just how much her compassionate words had meant to him.

"Clarissa Jean, your granny is surely looking down with pride overflowing in her heart at how you turned out. I know I'm mighty proud of you."

When Doc turned to leave, Rissa linked her arm in his and walked out, and the last thing Trace heard was her insisting he come to dinner the next evening as she reminded him he'd promised to cut back his long hours after the first of the year. Before they'd gotten far, she'd turned and motioned Trace to follow them as they'd made their way to Tori's room.

TRACE SAT IN the chair next to Tori's bed, holding her small, left hand in both of his and stroked her ring finger absently as he talked to her despite her unconscious state.

"Princess, I am so sorry I wasn't with you, I should have been there to protect you. I'll never forget the terror I felt when I knew someone had taken you. I swear to you, I lost at least a decade, hell maybe two, off my life at that moment." He took several deep breaths trying to center himself before he could continue.

"You really need to come back to me, princess, I need to explain some things to you—mainly that I wasn't trying to ignore you or gain distance. Quite the opposite, actually," he chuckled softly at the irony of the whole thing.

"I was trying to set up everything for an elaborate proposal. I want you to be my wife, and I had this whole romantic scenario worked out, and I was getting the ring from a fellow club member who is a jeweler... and... fuck... I'm so sorry." He laid his head on his forearm and let the tears fall.

He hoped there was at least some small part of Tori that had been listening. That on some level of her consciousness, she'd been tuned into him, and she would have heard his desperate words. He asked her to fight her way back to him, and when she finally squeezed his fingers, the feeling of relief that washed through him almost took his breath away. He froze and searched her sweet face for any flicker of response.

Watching as she seemed to make a Herculean effort to open her eyes, he simply waited. When she finally got them to flutter open, she quickly squeezed them back shut, and he heard her soft groan of pain. The sound tore at his heart and brought him to his feet.

"Hang on, baby, I'll get the nurse."

Just as he reached for the door, he heard her pleading words. "No, please don't leave me." Trace quickly shouted out the door without leaving the room and was back at her side within a few seconds. He was grateful that as soon as she'd felt his fingers softly caressing the sides of her face, she sighed and turned into his touch.

For the first time since he'd picked her up in the snow, she looked content and relaxed. She seemed to slowly slip back into a drowsy state between sleep and awake. He couldn't say he blamed her—no doubt that was easier than dealing with the flood of people who'd come storming into the room. Trace noticed the first thing Doc did when he entered the room was pull the shades closed and dim the lights.

"Damn nurses think sunlight is a fucking cure-all. You'd think they'd learn as often as I bitch at them about this. Patients wake up, their eyes are assaulted by the light, and it feels like lightning shooting through their brains. Hell, it sears their damned eyes." Turning to Tori he softened his tone. "Now, pretty lady, how about you give that awake thing another shot? The light won't stab your brain with hot swords, I closed the damned shades. That's it. Open those beautiful eyes and let me introduce myself." Doc's voice was so soothing, Trace had to blink to be sure it was really coming from the gruff old doctor he'd grown up visiting for everything from broken bones to the chicken pox.

Trace watch as Tori struggled to open her eyes again. When it appeared as though she focused on Doc's face, she smiled at the heavily lined face of the older man who was leaning over her. Trace smiled at her, knowing her simple response to the prickly old doctor had probably just earned her a friend for life. He listened as Doc spoke in a soft, gentle manner to her.

"That's a good girl. Now, can you tell me your name, dear?"

"Tori… um, well, actually it's Victoria… Victoria Paulson." Tori looked alarmed by the sound of her own voice. Trace didn't care that it sounded so broken, it was pure music to his ears. "Can I have a drink? My throat is so very dry."

Doc picked up a cup from the table beside her bed and held the straw to her lips. He let her have several sips before returning the cup to the tray of the rolling table over her bed.

"Well, you gave all your friends quite a fright, my dear." Leaning forward he whispered close to her ear, "And I'm not even going to go into the state your man has been in." Smiling at her, he asked her a few more questions, then turned to Trace, told him to keep it light and easy, and he'd be back in a few minutes.

Tori had heard all the conversation between Trace and the doctor, well, she'd heard the words, but she hadn't really tracked it because she was stuck on the elderly doctor's words…*My man? Did he really say that? Or did I dream that, too?*

When Trace turned back to her after the doctor had

left the room, Tori wasn't sure exactly what he was thinking because his face was such a contrast of emotions. When he moved to take her hands in his again, she wondered if she'd been dreaming earlier when she'd heard him talking about the plans he'd had for the evening. She wasn't sure whether she should ask or not, but finally decided she'd just take a small step.

"How long have you been here?"

"After I found you in the snow," Trace smiled, "I carried you to the ambulance, princess, and I have only left your side for fifteen minutes since then—when that demon dressed as a nurse ran me out, so they could settle you into this bed." He laughed softly and stroked her face. "It was touch and go for a while whether or not they were going to kick me out for the ruckus I raised. Thank God, the Lamonts basically built this place, and Zach was with me in the waiting room. His family connections and charm kept me from being booted."

When Tori's cheeks turned pink and she ducked her head, giving him a shy smile, he asked her, "What are you really wanting to know, princess?" He'd sensed she was dancing around what she was really trying to find out, and her expression had confirmed it. After everything she'd been through, she should know better than most people just how short life could be, and he hoped she'd be bold and not waste another second of it.

"Well, I am trying to decide if I dreamt what I heard because it was wishful thinking or if it was real." She tried to turn away from his intense look, but he held her chin easily with his fingers.

"It pleases me you think what you heard might be wishful thinking on your part. That bodes well for me getting the answer I want." He chuckled softly then continued, "Princess, if you heard me talking about my plans to ask you to be my wife, then you have it exactly right. I am so sorry you interpreted my nervousness as an attempt to distance myself from you." He shook his head, he couldn't believe how things had gone so horribly wrong.

"If it's any consequence, Mitch nearly took my head off about my deplorable behavior, and Bryant and Rissa have been running a close second and third. And that is without even mentioning Jenna who has been likened to the Tasmanian devil when she's riled up." Tori appeared to be surprised all his friends had taken up for her, but it warmed his heart to know she fit in so perfectly.

"I've spent most of life feeling like I was on the outside looking in, like I never really belonged anywhere, and now, everything seems to be falling into place. I've found a place to call home, friends, my own practice, and the man of my dreams. It's like all the pieces of a very large puzzle are finally falling into their rightful places." Tori blinked several times as if she'd just realized she'd been speaking out loud.

"Man of your dreams, huh? Damn, princess, I surely do wish you would give me an answer to my question." Blinking her eyes again as if trying to focus on him, she seemed lost in thought for a few seconds. He suspected her head was still fuzzy, and she seemed blissfully unaware of how torturous it was waiting for her to answer his damned question.

"I'm sorry, did I space out?"

"Tori, I'm just wondering about my proposal. I, well, I was wondering if you would do me the great honor of becoming my wife?" He pulled a small white leather box from his pocket and opened it, showing her the most dazzling ring she'd ever seen.

She looked at the ring and gasped, "Oh my God, Trace it's so lovely, but I'd marry you even if you used quarters at the gumball machines at the front of the grocery store to get me a ring." She looked up into his eyes and whispered, "I have no idea how this happened, but you owned my heart from the moment you locked me in that café office to keep me safe." She smiled at his stunned expression. "It's true... no man had ever done anything so gallant for me... ever. You made sure I was safe, then ran straight to the danger to try to help. Everything else was icing on a very sweet cake. Well, except the sex... and well..."

Tori was sure Trace wasn't about to let that sentence go unfinished because it could go so far in either direction. She held back her smile when he cocked his brow in question.

"Princess, I'd appreciate you finishing that sentence please before my curiosity gets the best of me."

She felt her face flame and knew it was a brilliant red, but she finally found her voice and answered.

"Well, the sex is just so incredible. Really, I had no idea it could even be that wonderful. There is just so much about it that is over-the-top perfect... well, could you maybe give me fifty or sixty years to come up with a way to explain it?"

Trace's smile was so blinding, she wondered for a minute if she had ever seen a man so handsome. She was humbled, yet again, by how she'd gotten so lucky to arrive in Climax just those few minutes late and how so many things had to have occurred in just the right sequence to get her to this point. She sent up a silent prayer of thanks to the sweet great-uncle she'd never even met who made it all possible.

Chapter 11

TRACE HADN'T WASTED any time sliding the large diamond ring on to her finger and herding his friends into her room to share in their joy and to celebrate. The nursing staff had nearly come unglued until Zach Lamont had once again worked his charm like a magic spell. Even Doc Woods had joined in when he'd stopped by to let them know her blood tests had revealed a common sedative, and as soon as he could get her discharge papers worked up, she'd be free to return home as long as she wouldn't be alone.

Assuring Doc his fiancée would indeed be closely monitored, Trace had immediately started making phone calls to ensure his friends completed the security check they'd planned to make in and around his house and the new perimeter alarms were ready. Colt Matthews was also making calls, arranging armed patrols, and distributing pictures of Gary George to just about everyone within a hundred miles in any direction.

Tori watched while the men fell over themselves with security concerns. She was grateful when Rissa made her way to her bedside and took her hand.

"Don't look so worried, sweet friend," Rissa whispered. "They are always like this when one of 'their women' is in danger. Jenna and I have been there, and I can tell you this is their regular MO for these types of circumstances." Tori couldn't help but smile when Rissa laughed. "I'd say you'll get used to it, but that would be a lie. But I can honestly say you're in good company! Kat, Jenna, and I can sympathize with you. I also knew it was possible you'd be released today, so I brought you some clothes." Rissa had snickered when Trace's face snapped to theirs in alarm. Tori smiled reassuringly at Trace when she heard Rissa say, "Don't worry, Trace, I've got it covered, you don't have to take your lovely fiancée out into a cold, Colorado January evening in that sexy little number she was wearing at The Club." Both women giggled at the relief in his eyes.

"Rissa, you are an angel. I hope those two knuckle-heads you're married to know what a treasure you are." Trace's warm words to Rissa touched Tori's heart. Just knowing he was a good guy to others was reassuring. Any man who was as genuinely sweet to everyone he knew couldn't be acting, he really was as wonderful as he appeared.

Tori nearly laughed out loud when Rissa boldly told Trace, "Well, feel free to share that information with them at every opportunity, cowboy because I keep telling them that very same thing, but it doesn't seem to make much of a dent sometimes." Rissa was obviously enjoying the glares she was getting from both Mitch and Bryant as they continued working on the logistics of Tori's return to the ranch. Tori snickered when Rissa smiled sweetly at them, and both men rolled their eyes, and even though they returned their attention to their phone conversations, they'd moved so they flanked their spit-fire wife.

Rissa looked at Trace and smiled. "I was just assuring Tori even though you are all going all 'Alpha Male' on her, your hearts are in the right place, and her safety really is at the heart of the issue."

It hadn't even occurred to Trace she might be over-whelmed by everything taking place in her room. He turned to her, concern etched in his expression.

"Princess, if this is too much right now, I understand. I promise you as soon as Doc gets your paperwork done, we'll get you out of here and go home, so you can get some rest."

Tori finally realized, at some time during the night, he had changed out of his leathers, and she was amazed at how sexy he looked in his faded blue jeans, sapphire-colored chamois shirt, and dark-brown cowboy boots. *It ought to be illegal for a man to look that hot. How am I supposed to rest when we get home when I'll be looking at him... dressed like that?*

He leaned close, and she couldn't help but inhale his clean scent. He smelled as if he had just showered with an underlying scent unique to him. Tori saw him smile when she leaned into him and inhaled deeply.

"Sweetness, you keep looking at me like that and I'm going to have to clear the room and fuck you before we leave. And as much appeal as that idea holds, I'm pretty sure the hospital staff wouldn't approve, and I'm not sure Zach could talk me out of the consequences." His words dripped with intent, and Tori felt her pussy gush with cream in preparation even though her mind knew it was going to be hours before he could fulfill his promise.

TRACE HAD SEEN Tori rouse a bit and knew she was vaguely aware they'd pulled to a stop in front of the ranch's main house, but she had drifted off again by the time he'd made his way around the truck and opened her door. He worried the cold air would startle her, but she barely stirred, another testament to how exhausted she was. Doc Woods had given him a twenty-minute lecture on how to care for her before finally conceding that, yes, he could always call the hospital if he had any questions.

Rissa had finally managed to distract the good doctor yet again while he made his escape, and Trace made a mental note to send a large gift basket to her for all her help and support. God only knows what would have happened last night if Rissa hadn't seen Tori go out of sight and sounded the alarm. Hell, he'd be in her debt forever for that alone.

Trace scooped Tori up into his arms and carried her gently up the front steps. Just as they approached the front door, it opened. The Lamonts' housekeeper and cook, Selita was standing alongside Mia Marshall and both women stepped aside to let them enter. Mia had re-married Dylan Marshall a few months ago, and Trace had to smile at her rounded belly. He'd been thrilled when they'd found love again. Mia had divorced Dylan a few years earlier in a misguided attempt to keep him safe when she was working a very dangerous case, but as a result of some very strange circumstances, lightning had struck twice, and they'd married again and were expecting their first child in a few months.

"Well, what a pleasant surprise." Looking at Selita he added, "Selita, I'll bet my kitchen smells like heaven on earth." The older Hispanic woman glowed at his kind words. Selita had worked for the Lamont family for the better part of three decades, and despite Trace's best efforts to lure her away, she had always turned him down, but she still kept him well supplied in frozen dinners. She made them in advance and sent several home with him whenever he visited the Lamonts.

"Mr. Trace, you are always tiger's roar for me. I just left you a few things, so you can spend your time caring for your beautiful wife-to-be and not making those Oscar dogs I saw in your icebox. Shame on you for eating those things. You should come to ShadowDance more, and I could keep you eating better." The tiny woman, known at Shadow-Dance as the Honduran Dynamo, was shaking her head in disgust at what she'd found in his refrigerator. Selita was well known for butchering common expressions, and sometimes, talking to her could be confusing, but more often it was just a hoot.

"Melita," Trace looked at Mia and smiled, "you are looking like one hot little mama. I'll bet your husband is over the moon about that sweet baby you are carrying." He knew for a fact Dylan Marshall was indeed thrilled he and Mia were finally expecting their first child—it had been a long time coming.

Dylan had never gotten over their divorce, and Trace always marveled at how openly affectionate the former agents were with one another. Dylan had retired due to an injury at the same time they'd divorced, and his move back home to Climax had been marked by a deep sadness. It wasn't until Mia had come back into his life anyone had seen the reappearance of the fun-loving man they'd grown up with.

When Trace returned to the kitchen after laying Tori on their bed and covering her with a well-worn quilt, he found several of his friends sitting around his dining room table. Jenna Lamont-Matthews stood and approached him, concern etching her beautiful face.

"Is she okay, Trace? We've all been worried sick about her. Does she need anything?"

Trace pulled her into a quick hug, patting her back in a brotherly move that brought a smile to the face of her husband who was sitting nearby. Colt Matthews knew Trace had been family friends with the Lamonts for as long as any of them could remember, and Trace could tell the former Special Forces Team Leader was secure in his relationship with his beautiful bride. It was something Trace was grateful for because it would have been very difficult to change the way he'd interacted with Jenna their whole lives.

"You are a sweetheart for asking, but I can't think of a thing she needs, but if you are still here when she wakes up, please feel free to ask her." Then addressing the entire group, he added, "Doc assures me she will fully recover, but it will take a few days for the drug she was given to fully be fully flushed from her system. She was very lucky it was a mild dose since she isn't a large woman, and it was a pretty powerful sedative. I will be watching her closely for any signs of PTSD, but honestly, my main concern right now is how to keep this from happening again."

"I want you to know we'll all do everything we can," Colt spoke up first. "Alex and Zach have authorized the use of any ShadowDance resource to help, so we'll be providing electronics security upgrades until you can get your system up and fully functional. We'll also be providing staff both inside and outside your residence. We've already spent some time educating your ranch hands and making sure they are all aware of the situation and exactly what's at stake."

Sheriff Dylan Marshall spoke up next. "I've got patrols in the area as much as possible, and my deputies are canvassing the town to find out if anyone has had any dealings with someone matching Gary George's description. We are also leaving copies of his picture with everyone we talk to and making sure they understand how important it is they let us know if they see him." Dylan had made it clear earlier in the day he was fed up with women being hurt in his jurisdiction, and he was going to do everything he could to find out who had hired the flunky they'd caught after Tori was drugged and taken from the club.

Trace swallowed past the lump in his throat as he looked around the room. It took him a few seconds to calm the emotions racing through him, so he could thank his friends for their help and assure them Tori would be just as touched by their love and concern as he was. As he finished speaking, he looked up to see her standing in the doorway with tears glistening in her eyes.

"Princess, what are you doing up already? And why the tears, sweetness?"

She padded toward him, her sock covered feet silently crossing the room until she leaned into him, and he wrapped her in his arms. She finally looked up.

"I'm just so touched that your friends love you so much, they are willing to go to all this trouble just because I'm marrying you and…"

No one had seen Alex Lamont arrive, but he quickly made himself known when he cut her words off. "Victoria, that's quite enough of that nonsense. We are very close to Trace, that's true enough, but we are your friends as well, and as you are soon going to discover, we take care of our own. Now, someone update me on the progress. I've got a very pregnant, impossibly cranky wife at home, and I need to get back there. I've left Zach in charge of her and things being how they are, she'll have him twisted into a pretzel and have gotten him to agree to God knows what if I leave them alone for too long." His low chuckle and smile took most of the sting out of his words, and Tori had to smile at him.

It was plain to see Alex Lamont worshipped his fireball of a wife. It had been his love for his family that had been the first thing Tori had noticed about the man who now seemed every bit the soldier she'd been told he had once been.

After several people in the room gave Alex updates, he offered several suggestions and reiterated his orders to the members of the ShadowDance staff and said his goodbyes. Tori was impressed with the economy of his movements and the smooth way he handled all the information he'd been given.

Tori had watched as he processed everything he was being told as if he was gathering military intelligence and quickly set a plan in motion. She had to smile to herself when she'd been able to easily identify his former Special Forces team members simply by watching the way they responded to his inquiries and orders.

Standing in the kitchen in the soft yoga pants and off-the-shoulder sweater Rissa had brought her, she thought, judging by everyone's stunned expressions, she must look a fright and unconsciously tried to smooth down her crazy curls. Trace's large hand stopped her movements.

"You look beautiful, and I want you to stop worrying about what others think." He turned her in his arms, so they were facing each other, placed his hands on her waist, picked her up as if she weighed nothing at all, and sat her on the counter, so their faces were closer together, and spoke against her ear.

"You are the most beautiful woman in the entire world, always remember that. I want you to know that I'm drawn to your inner beauty as well as what others can see on the outside. You are my other half, sweetheart, and I will do everything in my power to prove that to you each and every day for the rest of my life."

Tori thought her heart would burst with the joy Trace brought to her heart. She felt as if he had reached deep into her soul. As he had from the moment they met, Trace had figured out exactly what she needed, and then handed it to her on a silver platter. She'd spent her entire life trying to be better... do more... prove herself in all things, and to have a man like Trace tell her she was everything to him was just more than she could have ever asked for.

Once again, Tori found herself thanking the Universe for the gift standing in front of her. She felt like she was quickly running out of steam and had been thinking about going back upstairs to rest when she found herself suddenly lost in thought.

Trace was studying her closely, looking deeply into her eyes, and she wondered if he sensed her internal battle. She was trying to decide which was more important, her desire to be polite to their guests or her overwhelming fatigue. He was watching the play of emotions move across her face when suddenly, her stomach growled so loud, he leaned his head back and laughed out loud.

"Selita, do we have anything for my lovely fiancée to eat? It seems she's a bit hungry even though she wouldn't dream of *mentioning* it."

Chapter 12

TORI HAD EATEN a light dinner, then excused herself, so she could return upstairs for a long soaking bath. Trace had helped her get settled and returned downstairs to see their guests out. Jamie Creed had remained inside but had assured Trace he didn't need anything, and he should return to Tori.

Trace was grateful to the Lamonts for lending him one of their best. Jamie had been a SEAL team sniper, and even though Trace didn't actually see a weapon, it was a given the man was heavily armed. It was equally likely he'd already stashed loaded weapons all over the house. Trace made a mental note to mention that to Tori and hoped she wouldn't be put off by it. Trace stood silently at the top of the stairs and watched the younger man for several minutes. *Christ, he moves like a fucking cat, sleek and silent.*

Alex and Zach did contract work for the various governments on occasion, and Jamie Creed was on almost every team they put together. Men trained at Shadow-Dance disappeared for a few weeks, then slid right back into a routine as if they'd never been gone. Trace had laughed more than once at how the whole operation seemed to fly right under the radar of most of the residents of Climax where, typically, the local busybodies didn't miss a single thing.

Trace hadn't realized he was still watching Jamie until the man spoke to him without even turning around.

"Bra, you gonna just stand there all night watching me or you gonna go to your woman?"

Jamie's Cajun slang was always entertaining and managed to attract any number of the submissives on the occasions the lanky young man visited the club's busy main lounge. Smiling to himself, Trace shook his head at how spooky it was the man sensed his presence without turning in his direction.

Knowing Jamie had the downstairs secured, Trace turned silently and went on up the stairs to where he knew Tori was still soaking in a bubble bath. Looking in on her, he wasn't surprised when he saw that her eyes were closed, but he could see her sexy smile and knew she was enjoying the music he'd started downstairs. One of his favorite features of the beautiful log home he'd built was the stereo system. The equipment was state-of-the-art, and he'd made certain it streamed to every room throughout the entire house. There were even speakers on each deck and in various places throughout the pool area and front porch. Trace might be a rancher, but he loved beautiful music. His mother had been an accomplished pianist, and he'd grown up knowing the power of music to soothe or excite the soul.

Stepping back into the bedroom, Trace lit candles, then slipped out of his clothes and re-entered the bathroom. He carefully slipped behind Tori in the large tub, set the jets to rewarm, and begin moving the water around them in slow swirls that would soothe her tired muscles. Trace wanted to make sure she got every bit of rest she could. He'd also been pushing her to drink a lot of liquids, just as Doc had ordered. They wanted to flush the drugs from her system as quickly as possible.

The large marble tub he'd installed in the master bath was a sharp contrast to the bathrooms in Mitch and Bryant's cabin. For each rustic element the other men implemented, Trace had gone equally far in the other direction, choosing modern sleek lines. The irony hadn't been lost on any of them as they'd helped each other with the designs.

The soldier and engineer had gone for natural and rustic, and the rancher had gone to the other extreme, opting for as modern a look as he could get. The black-and-white marble gleamed in the soft light, and Trace smiled when Tori moaned in contentment.

"Princess, you feel so good pressed against me. Feeling your warmth flush against me, skin to skin is nearly perfect." For several minutes, he soaked up the feeling of her in his arms. He knew better than most people how lucky he was to have this second chance with Tori. He'd nearly lost her to the lunatic who didn't seem to understand the word no, and he swore to himself that he'd spend the rest of his life protecting her.

GARY GEORGE SAT in the Shift Captain's office, wondering how the hell things had gone so wrong. He had made it home from Colorado an hour before being called in and questioned for hours by the Internal Affairs clucks about an "attempted kidnapping" in Colorado. He'd explained that he had been on days off and had been working alone in his garage's large wood shop, so no, he didn't have anyone to vouch for him as to his whereabouts for the previous few days.

Next time, he wouldn't hire some fucking kid to bring the bitch to him. He also silently vowed the next time he got his hands on her, it wasn't going to be a fucking picnic for her either. *You think your dog died an ugly death, bitch, just wait until you see what I have planned for you.*

Apparently, Miss Victoria Paulsen had made some powerful friends since she'd moved to *Colorful Colorado*. Judging by the black suits now chatting up his Captain down the hall, he'd say it was damned likely she'd hooked up with someone who had well-connected Fed friends. If he survived this witch hunt, he'd lie low for a couple of months, then he'd go back and finish what he'd started. Nobody walked away from him and lived to tell about it, well, not for long, anyway.

Being a cop was the perfect cover. Hell, he'd even worked most of the cases involving the women he had killed, and no one had ever suspected his involvement. Movement on the other side of the glass wall brought him back to the moment. When he saw his supervisor shake hands with the Feds and smile as the other two men walked back down the hall toward the exit, he knew he'd dodged the bullet... again.

SITTING IN THEIR rental car down the street from the Houston precinct where Gary George worked, both agents watched as he left the building. His smile and the cocky walk only confirmed the impression they'd gotten as they'd watched his interview earlier in the day. And after talking with his Captain, they were all convinced the man they were dealing with had likely been involved in many if not all the unsolved murders of several women in the city during the past few years. They'd been working what everyone suspected was a serial killer case for almost a year, and the one common thread was Officer Gary George. Now, all they had to do was prove it.

When Alex Lamont had called them yesterday, they'd almost rejoiced at the excuse to get closer to their prime suspect. After making certain Alex had a good understanding of the seriousness of the situation, they'd called Captain Gasman to enlist his help. Sitting in a small, remote observation room, they'd watched the interview via live stream from various hidden cameras in the Internal Affairs office's interview room.

It had only taken a few short minutes for Captain Gasman to recognize several problems with the man he had only minutes before defended and described as an exemplary employee. The inconsistencies in the officer's answers were so small, anyone who hadn't worked with the man for a long time would have missed them.

The agents had been impressed with Gasman's astute observations and his willingness to be open-minded enough to recognize a serious problem within his ranks. Everyone would be watching George for the foreseeable future. They had all agreed he would likely take a breather and wait for the heat of the situation to dissipate before resuming his pursuit of Victoria Paulson. George would know this had been a close call, so now, it was just a matter of waiting him out and not letting their guard down.

Relaxing in the passenger seat as they watched George saunter down the sidewalk looking, for all intents and purposes, like he had the world by the tail, Agent Rivera called Alex Lamont with an update and promised to visit soon. Joe Rivera and his partner, Derek Lake had been Navy SEALs and worked with the Lamonts on joint missions on several occasions. Even though they hadn't been on the same team, they had a mutual respect for each other. The adage "Once a SEAL, always a SEAL" was common knowledge for a reason, so they looked forward to visiting the Lamonts' Club sometime…soon!

Chapter 13

HOLDING TORI IN the whirlpool was as close to heaven on earth as Trace figured he'd ever get, and Trace knew just exactly how to make it perfect for her as well. Slowly moving his hands up to her shoulders, he massaged them gently until he felt her muscles go lax under his work-roughened hands.

"Turn around, princess. I want to feel your lovely breasts against my chest, and I want to be able to look into your beautiful eyes as I sink my cock deep inside your sweet heat."

Trace could practically feel the shift in her energy as she repositioned herself in his lap. Looking deep into her eyes, he watched as they dilated with her arousal. As he shifted, so he could slide into her tight pussy, he watched the base of her throat and saw the exact moment her pulse and respiration rates accelerated.

"Are you wet for me, my little snow angel?" *Oh my God in Heaven, I may not survive this woman. She already owns my heart and soul.*

There was a good chance his cock was going to erupt like fucking Mt. Vesuvius as he rubbed the engorged head over the swollen lips of her labia. The feel of her heated flesh slipping along his own was the most amazing moment of anticipation he'd ever experienced. Hell, Trace wasn't sure who he was tormenting more, and soon it was more than he could take. He pushed in so deep, he felt the head of his cock bump Tori's cervix.

With his deep plunge, he heard her gasp just before she moaned his name, "Trace...oh my God... Yes." He watched in absolute awe as she leaned back into the water. Her new position would cause a shift in pressure and intensity as his rigid length passed over her sweet spot. When she shuddered, signaling she was rapidly approaching the point of no return, his entire body responded. Remembering the night she'd told him she shuddered because it always felt as if lightning was racing up her spine had him fighting to remain in control.

And there it was—the tipping point. Trace watched her back bow as if she'd been hoisted by an invisible line tied around her torso. God, he loved watching as she lost herself in the pleasure and wave after wave of pure ecstasy washed over her sweet face.

Trace wondered if he could maintain his control when Tori moved fractionally, shifting to the perfect angle for the head of his cock to rub the spongy spot at the front of her channel. He nearly came himself when her pussy clamped down on him like a vise. The feeling of being squeezed by hot, wet velvet was almost more than he could take, and holding off had been an exercise in sheer willpower.

The channel of her pussy flexed and squeezed in a primal mating rhythm as old as time, and Trace felt Tori's ecstasy as her climax peaked several times in rapid succession. When she finally began to come back down from the highest point of her pleasure, he was enraptured by the look of sated bliss that passed over her beautiful face. Everything about her touched him so deeply, he felt tears build and had to quickly blink them away. *Great way to show her what a strong Dom you are—cry just watching her come, geez, Bartell, get a fucking grip.*

When he'd finally regained enough emotional control to speak, he simply said, "Beautiful." Tori's sweet smile was followed by another intense flex of her vaginal walls that immediately redirected his attention to where he was still buried deep inside her heat. Just as he was about to move, he saw goose bumps spread over her softly rounded abdomen and knew he would have to wait until she was dry and warm in his bed before he found his own release.

"You're cold, come on, princess, let's get you out of this water, dried, and warmed up. And then I'm going to make sweet love to you." He knew she was ready to argue, but he covered her lips with his own and kissed her as he stood and stepped from the water. Grabbing a towel from the warming bar, he wrapped her in its plush warmth.

MOVING TO THE bedroom after they were both dry, Tori soon found herself being lowered onto the softest bed she'd ever slept on. It was like laying on a cloud. Looking up into Trace's face, she lost herself in his eyes and knew she would never find another man she would love more.

The speed at which they had recognized love in each other still shocked her. Bringing her hand up to caress the side of his face, she felt herself being carried away on a wave of desire that would only be satisfied when she knew he'd lost himself in her body just as she'd lost herself in his a few minutes ago. The strength of her earlier orgasm had surprised her. She hadn't been ready for the depth of the connection between them and had fought the tears that had threatened to fall. *Oh yeah, Tori, way to turn a hot guy on, cry when he gives you the best orgasm of your entire life.*

"What was that thought, sweetness? And I want to caution you about trying to edit your response. Don't ever lie to me because I promise you, I'll know."

Trace was watching her eyes so closely, there was no way he'd miss the flash of self-recrimination she knew had moved through her. He'd told her he knew it would take a long time to reprogram her thinking, and she wondered if he knew it might well take the rest of their lives to get it done.

"Well, I was just thinking that, well... our connection is so strong for some reason I can't even begin to understand or explain and well... we just seem to click so perfectly. And, well, I don't want to mess it up. I seem to be awfully good at messing things up... and... oh, damn... that didn't really make any sense, did it?"

TRACE NOTICED TORI wouldn't even look at him now. She obviously wasn't used to having anyone who genuinely cared about her feelings. He didn't want her to worry her answer had gone too far—there would never be a time she shared too much of herself with him. It was critical that she understood how important her honesty was and how much deeper their bond would be if they were completely open with one another.

He was saddened to know she'd never been with anyone who asked or honestly cared about how she felt. Trace wanted her to know he would not only ask, but he would actually listen to her answers as well. He would always listen to her with his ears and his heart, and it was apparent to him, she simply wasn't accustomed to that sort of intense attention—*yet*.

"Princess, look at me." When she didn't look up at him, he shifted from lying alongside her, so he was lying over her, cradled between her legs. Holding himself up enough, she had no choice but to look at him as he cupped his large hands along the sides of her flushed face. "And? Finish it, Victoria. There will be no secrets between us. I won't allow it." His tone had taken on more of what she would recognize as his Dom tone. It was the voice her body responded to—usually before her mind had a chance to process the words.

Trace hadn't planned to top her tonight, but he could see Tori was struggling. She was trying to back away emotionally, but he was going to rope her and bring her right back to his heart, using the role she seemed to respond to without even thinking.

When she looked up into his face, he prayed she would see her own strength of spirit reflected in his eyes because it was there... she just needed to recognize it. He knew his patience would be rewarded when she took a deep breath.

"I was just thinking that I was so completely flattened by the connection I felt during the orgasm I had a few minutes ago and... well, I... I almost cried because it was so deep, and I knew if I did, well, what a turnoff would tears be?"

He smiled down at her because she had spit it all out so fast, and now, she looked like a very pretty balloon someone had poked a small hole in, appearing to be slowly deflating right in front of him—okay, right beneath him—*whatever*.

"Oh, my love, I felt it as well and had to pull myself back from that very same edge. Rest assured, sweetheart, I'll never be turned off by your tears. I will celebrate the tears of joy, mourn your tears of sadness, and I'll treasure the ones that are just meant to tell me I've touched your soul." His lips brushed over hers in a sweet press of warmth intended to melt her heart.

"The tears that let me know I've rocked your world are the sweetest ones of all, and I'll be honored when you trust me enough to let me see those. If you have had a bad day and just feel like crying to vent all that frustration, I'll hold you and kiss away the tears that fall. I want it all, princess. Every little piece of you is important to me."

Moving so the head of his cock poised at the entrance to her heat, he watched her eyes fill with tears and smiled when she let them stream down her temples. Leaning to each side, he kissed the tear tracks and whispered sweet words of love into her ear as he slid deep into her tight pussy. He told her how amazing her cunt felt as it pulled him deeper with each stroke. Trace had always loved being a Dominant when it came to sex, but right at this moment, he wasn't sure there was anything better than just making sweet love to the woman in his arms.

Tori found herself completely lost in the magic of the moment, her body racing unabated to the very cusp of release, but she couldn't seem to grasp it.

"Oh please... it's so close, but I can't... it's so very close... why can't I get it?" Tori didn't realize she had spoken the words aloud until Trace answered her.

"Oh, princess, you are so fucking perfect for me. You can't get there with straight vanilla sex, can you? Fuck me, but you are the most amazing woman on the planet, and you are mine. *All mine!* Let me show you the way, princess." Pulling from her depths, Trace quickly flipped her over and pulled her ass high in the air before plunging in again. He set a pounding pace and just as he reached around her and pinched her swollen clit, he whispered in her ear, "Come for me, my love."

The words had no sooner left his lips than he felt her shatter beneath him and took him with her. Trace's body stiffened, and he'd have sworn colored fireworks were shooting off behind his eyelids as the heat of his release splashed back onto the head of his cock after bathing her cervix in his seed. He felt an unexplainable primal sense of satisfaction knowing he'd planted his seed deep within the woman he loved. Someday soon, he hoped they would begin the family they often talked about late in the evening as they'd watched the dying embers fade in the fireplace.

Trace would always treasure the time they'd spent as friends while becoming lovers because those hours had provided a foundation of trust they'd both needed, and he was sure that foundation would help their marriage hold up to the daily strain relationships endured just as a part of living together.

Finding a woman who was strong enough to submit was a blessing beyond any Trace had ever even been brave enough to pray for. And having Tori wrapped in his arms was just about the best feeling in the world.

"Princess, you are a gift sent straight from heaven. I have no clue what I could have ever done that would put me in such good graces with the Universe above, but I am grateful beyond measure. You belong to me, and no one hurts what's mine."

Tori gasped when Trace's cock went from semi-erect to rock hard while still buried inside her. Brushing his fingertips in slow circles over her temples, he told her, "I'm going to keep myself inside you as we go to sleep because I want you to know in the most basic way, you belong to me, sweetheart."

Rolling them to their sides with his cock still buried deep inside her, he felt her shudder as his possessive words of ownership sunk in, and he felt as if a radiant joy had settled deep in his heart as she settled against him in acceptance. He knew the instant she let sleep take her, and when he knew she was deeply asleep, he let slumber claim him as well. Just before nodding off, Trace remembered Jamie Creed was keeping watch in the house. The other man had likely heard them both cry out their release, and Trace's inner caveman was filled with a ridiculous sense of pride.

Jamie Creed had been walking through the Bartell ranch house when he'd heard the unmistakable sound of flesh slapping flesh just before he'd heard Trace speaking softly, then Tori's scream. Smiling to himself, he silently cheered his friend on. He couldn't think of anyone who deserved happiness more than Trace Bartell, and even though there was just a small piece of him that wished he could find a woman who would fit him as perfectly, he also knew karma was going to be a bitch for him.

There wasn't any way to paint it that didn't look bleak. His years as a sniper had put a lot of black marks on his soul. Would he ever find a woman who could deal with the darkness he'd seen and done? Would he recognize her if she showed up on his doorstep?

Somehow, he doubted it, but he also remembered the

words Rissa had spoken to him New Year's Eve before the whole party had gone FUBAR. She'd slipped up beside him and squeezed his hand. "She's out there. You'll see, and when she walks into your life, you'll feel your whole world shift on its axis."

When he'd looked down at the beautiful, pint-sized, green-eyed pixie, he'd been humbled by the sincerity painting her sweet face. Then she'd stood up on her tiptoes and kissed his cheek and whispered, "Happy New Year, Jamie" before turning on her heel and walking back into her husband's arms. Bryant Davis had looked up and smiled at him with a knowing look then hugged her tightly to his chest, and Jamie had felt like she'd handed him a gift box filled with hope for a future he had barely allowed himself to even dream possible.

Chapter 14

Four Months Later

"OH MY GOD, they are so amazing. And it was nice of you to have three, so we could each hold one at the same time." Rissa was sitting in the wooden rocker in the baby suite with little Christopher Lamont resting comfortably on her own growing baby bump.

Kat Lamont handed baby Daniel to his Aunt Jenna who quickly snuggled him against her neck and started pacing the room.

"Sure," Jenna laughed, "give me the one who always has to be on the move to be happy." Kat smiled at her best friend and sister-in-law because she knew Jenna's words were pure jest... Jenna adored all three babies.

"Well, I'm no dummy, and I'm exhausted, but don't tell my husbands, or I'll never get to leave this damned house." Kat sighed and started to close her eyes until she heard a sound behind her.

"Language, Katarina, and I will have you know Zach and I are already well aware of how exhausted you are. Falling fast asleep during dinner was a pretty big clue, love." Alex moved around her to take his sweet daughter, Mary Catherine from her mama's tired arms. Looking at the baby's pink cheeks and softly curling strawberry blonde hair, he nuzzled her neck and started talking to her as if she were full grown rather than six weeks old.

"You are going to be a daddy's girl, aren't you, sweetheart? You are going to be the cooperative one, too, I can already tell." As he moved to stand near one of the large windows, he looked up at the others in the room and noted they were all staring at him as if he'd grown another head. "What?" he said, irritated they obviously thought his sweet words were out of character. *Damn, don't they know my heart melts every time I pick up any of my children?*

He reluctantly admitted Mary Kate, as she was already being called, had stolen his heart and soul the minute she had burst forth into the world. She'd been the first and had been screaming at the top of her lungs until the nurse had handed the screeching bundle to him, and miraculously, she had instantly gone completely silent, staring directly into his eyes. And as if deeming him worthy in less than a heartbeat, she had settled down and gone quickly to sleep. It had continued to be like that each time she was upset. Her beautiful mama could be at her wit's end and all either he or Zach had to do was pick up their daughter, and she was immediately content. Both of the boys seemed to favor a woman's touch. *Smart boys, our sons!*

Just as Alex was about to set her back in her cradle, Zach walked in followed by Trace and Tori. "I'll take her Royal Highness," Zach said as he scooped her up before she'd even made contact with the mattress. "Hey, baby girl, you weren't going to be happy just lying there were you? No, you'd rather have one of your devoted daddies holding you, wouldn't you, little princess?"

Tori made her way to Kat and sat next to her exhausted and frazzled-looking friend, reaching out to take Kat's small hand.

"How are you doing? Anything I can do to help you?" And then looking around the room, she smiled. "It looks like you have a lot of baby holders on hand already. So maybe something a bit more practical... like smuggled-in chocolates and ice cream?" With those words, she lifted a sack with a wicked grin.

The Lamonts' home had actually been Trace and Tori's second stop after returning from their honeymoon. Tori had insisted they make a quick detour to the local market. She'd wanted to pick up a couple of her friend's favorite treats. Tori had seen new mothers reeling before and had a feeling Kat would be feeling the strain of caring for three infants despite all the help surrounding her.

"Oh my God, you are an angel. Give me a hand up, and we'll escape to the kitchen. I really need a little space, and I'd like nothing more than a little adult conversation that didn't center on babies." As Tori helped Kat up, they quickly made their way down the winding stairs, leaving the others to watch out for the triplets for a while. As they sat at the counter, enjoying their treats, Tori smiled.

"So, tell me how you are really doing. You look like you're strung mighty tight for someone who is obviously exhausted. It's okay, I'm a lawyer and secrets are my specialty, so spill it."

Tori had noted the new mother was skating right on the edge of her sanity the minute they'd stepped in the room. She'd been grateful for the excuse to get her sweet friend alone, so they could chat. Kat had been a wonderful sounding board and had helped Tori understand being a victim of a crime was a blip on the radar compared to the longer process of healing. Kat, Jenna, and Rissa had all stressed that seeing herself as a victim was far too limiting, and there was far greater power in viewing herself as a survivor.

The tears that rolled down Kat's cheeks startled Tori into moving to embrace her friend in a warm hug. She didn't ask for explanations, just held her as Kat cried silently on her shoulder. Several minutes later, Kat drew back and hiccupped before smiling up at Tori's concerned face.

"I'm sorry, it's just that I can't let it out with anyone else because they freak out. Do you know Alex called a psychiatrist the first time I cried after the triplets were born? I kid you not... I was mortified! I tried to explain it's the hormones, but he and Zach are just so... well, they're so... Hell, I don't even have any words to explain it."

Tori's hearty laugh caused Kat to look up in surprise, but then suddenly she looked as if she'd really thought about what she'd said and started to giggle. Before either of them knew it, they are nearly falling off their seats, they were laughing so hard. When they finally seemed to get themselves under control, Kat looked up her with appreciation in her eyes.

"Oh, Tori, I can't tell you how good that felt. I haven't been able to vent all that pent-up emotion, and it was about to eat me up. You're the best... ice cream, chocolates, a good cry, and laughter. Damn... it just doesn't get any better than that."

"Oh, I'm so goooood!" She stood and danced a little jig before sitting back down and grinning at Kat. "I didn't have to say a single word. Just laughed at your speech problem and all's well. Damn, I think I missed my calling." Smiling brightly at her friend, she exaggerated her grunt of pain when Kat smacked her on the arm.

Tori made a mental note to check on her new friend regularly and watch her closely for symptoms of postpartum depression. After working with a young mother who had abandoned her young son after suffering from an acute case of postpartum fueled by the very real hormone imbalance Kat had just mentioned, Tori had learned the disorder affected more new mothers than not but was still widely misunderstood, and even more often, it went undiagnosed.

They spent the next few minutes catching up, Tori telling Kat all about the honeymoon trip she and Trace had just returned from. Tori told her if it had been up to her, they'd still be sunning themselves on the beaches of Aruba, but Trace had needed to get back because calving season was rapidly approaching.

Kat complained she hadn't had sex in months and if her husbands didn't take care of that soon, she was going to start interviewing surrogates. Tori had laughed but thought her friend's humorous words were likely, at the very least, partially based in truth. Tori asked about Jenna's return to school and Rissa's pregnancy. She'd been fascinated when Kat explained several members of The Club's security detail had just returned from a Black Ops mission.

The two of them had great fun letting their imaginations run wild, conjuring up all the circumstances, each one trying to be more outrageous in their imagined details than the other until they were nearly hysterical once again. When they'd finally somewhat recovered, they looked up to see Alex, Zach, and Trace standing just inside the room, looking at them as if they'd lost their minds. When she and Kat looked from the men's confused faces back to each other, they fell right into another fit of giggles.

"Damn," Zach chuckled and spoke just loud enough for his brother and lifelong friend to hear, "I love seeing her laugh again. It's been too long, and I was really starting to worry about her." Turning to Trace he added, "Thanks for bringing Tori over. It looks like she's made progress where the rest of us have failed." Trace thought his heart was going to burst with pride at his friend's appreciation of his new bride.

"She is amazing. I can't begin to tell you how much I love and appreciate her. It's like she was made just for me, you know? Honestly, I don't know how else to describe it. But I can damn sure tell you it humbles me that she agreed to become my wife." Trace might have been talking to his friends, but his gaze never left the amazing woman who pledged her life to him. *Damn, but I love the sound of that word… Wife! I still can't believe she is really my wife.*

Walking over, so he was standing alongside Tori, Trace leaned forward and kissed her forehead. "Well, now that you have set Kat up for a sugar-induced coma, we'd better be heading back to the ranch. I'd like to get back in time to check the heifers before turning in, and it looks like the skies are getting ready open up." Just then a brilliant flash of lightning lit up the room, followed almost immediately by a deafening crack of thunder. Alex and Zach shouted their goodbyes over their shoulders as they bolted up the stairs just as the cries of three frightened babies filled the air.

Trace watched as Tori gave Kat a long hug and made her promise to cut herself some slack and call if she needed anything even if it was just to talk. They watched as Kat made her way up the elegant staircase that looked like it had been taken right out of one of the mansions in *Gone with the Wind*. Trace thought about how quickly Tori and Kat had bonded as friends and how pleased he was she seemed to feel right at home in Climax after such a short time. After everything Tori had shared with him, he understood how she had always longed to feel the sense of belonging he often took for granted. His friends had been wonderful, and he was grateful to them for making her feel so welcome.

The wistful look on Tori's face didn't escape his notice, and he sent up a silent prayer he'd be able to fulfill every wish and dream he'd seen move through her eyes as she'd watched her friend heading back upstairs to join her family.

"Come on, sweetheart, we'd better get headed out before the weather turns too bad." Trace grabbed her hand, and they made a mad dash for his truck and were just pulling onto the highway when the rain started pounding down.

GARY GEORGE SAT across the highway, hidden by the trees, and watched as Tori and Trace Bartell turned and headed back in the direction of his ranch. He'd been supremely pissed off when he'd discovered she'd married the rancher and was gone on her honeymoon after he'd driven all the way to Colorado last week. He'd be paying them a visit real soon, but not tonight.

The rain would make the back-way onto their place impassable in a very short time. He wanted to get in, get her, and get out as quickly as possible. He'd taken a leave of absence when he'd feigned a back injury and wasn't supposed to report back to work for another couple of weeks, so he had plenty of time to wait out the rain and muddy roads.

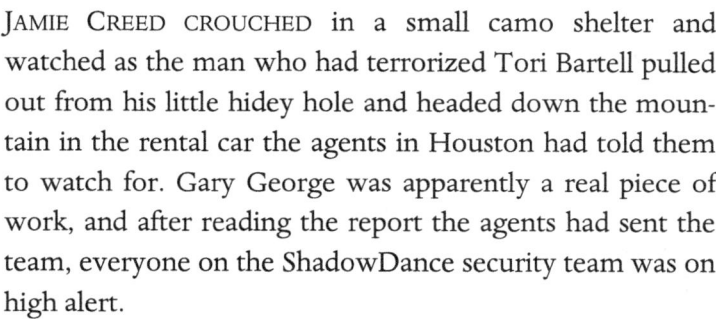

JAMIE CREED CROUCHED in a small camo shelter and watched as the man who had terrorized Tori Bartell pulled out from his little hidey hole and headed down the mountain in the rental car the agents in Houston had told them to watch for. Gary George was apparently a real piece of work, and after reading the report the agents had sent the team, everyone on the ShadowDance security team was on high alert.

He'd been in the Crow's Nest when the call came in several days ago, so Jamie had time to get several observation points set up before the piece of shit had even made it to town. The new security systems at the club, Trace's ranch, and the cabin were all fully functional. Jamie was confident no one was going to be moving anywhere near any of those properties without alerting the entire security team. He quickly sent out a text to each member of the team, detailing his observations, so everyone would exercise every precaution.

Damn, he was glad it looked like things were finally going to move toward resolution. The past few months of anticipation had begun to wear damned thin. *You're going down, fucker. You're not killing anyone on my watch. You think you're invincible? Bring it, asshat.*

Chapter 15

TRACE FELT HIS phone vibrate in his pocket just as they had pulled onto the highway after leaving Shadow-Dance Mountain. The rain made driving damned dangerous in the mountains, and he wasn't about to endanger them or anyone else by taking his attention away from the road to read a message. After he and Tori checked the heifers in the pasture behind the calving barn, they'd returned home, and he'd carried her over the threshold again despite her protests the third time was really over the top.

Moving quickly to the bedroom, he couldn't help wondering if he'd ever tire of the warm feeling of contentment carrying his wife in his arms brought to his heart. They'd arrived home so late last night, they had both fallen into bed and been asleep within seconds. The ranch hands had called with questions shortly after dawn, so he was impatient to get Tori naked and under him.

He was going to fuck her until they were both satisfied, and he warned her that was going to take most of the night. He couldn't help but smile as he remembered how her cheeks had flushed as he'd told her all the ways he planned to make her come. That she'd endured so much and retained that level of innocence was about the sexiest thing he'd ever seen. As he rounded the corner of their bedroom, his heart nearly burst with gratitude for his friends Dylan and Mia Marshall. The room was awash in the soft glow of candlelight, and the sounds of soft piano music wafted from the ceiling speakers. Dylan had called him earlier and told him they'd be using the key Trace had left with them for the house because Mia wanted to "create a mood" for them. For a couple of former DEA agents, they were a romantic pair.

Several weeks earlier, Trace had asked Mia to spend some time with Tori, teaching her some basic self-defense moves and giving her small-weapons training. Trace had loved seeing how quickly the two women had become friends. Tori seemed to have a magical way of drawing people to her.

Trace had only looked at his phone a few times while they'd been on their honeymoon, and he hadn't yet told her that Gary George had taken a leave of absence and left Texas. He'd wanted her to be able to enjoy their trip without losing herself in fear, but he was going to have to tell her soon. Damn, he dreaded seeing the fear he knew was going to cloud her beautiful eyes.

Trace set Tori on her feet in their bedroom and looked at her in the soft candlelight. Cupping her heart-shaped face between his palms, he poured his love for her into his kiss. Brushing his lips lightly over hers, he savored the sweet taste of her plump lips, and her scent surrounded him. Hell, kissing her was his new favorite pastime. Pushing between her parted lips, his tongue pushed forward, exploring her mouth with a growing urgency he was having trouble holding back.

"Oh, my sweet wife, I don't even know how to begin to tell you how much I love you and how blessed I feel to have found you." Trace pulled her into his arms and hugged her close, burying his face in her hair. Taking his time, he took several deep breaths, inhaling the citrus and sage scent that seemed to be her signature fragrance.

"You smell like a warm summer day. I could so easily lose myself in every little detail that is you." He pulled back and turned her toward the bathroom. "Take a few minutes and get yourself ready, but I want you back in this room within ten minutes—naked and laying on your back in the center of our bed." Trace was letting just enough of his Dom persona shine through to kick up her apprehension. He'd discovered that small bit of unease was a direct trigger for her arousal.

She responded beautifully to direct instruction and clearly stated expectations. They had agreed to work her slowly into a more intense D/s relationship, and she had promised she would let him know as soon as she felt she had reached her maximum level of comfort. Trace had explained that one of the hallmarks of a D/s partnership was the Dom always pushed the sub to expand their boundaries, but he never wanted to cross the line of what she could tolerate. Tori had chosen "uncle" as her safe word. They'd both laughed at the word's double meaning—her inheritance from an uncle had brought her to Colorado, and of course, the word's usual slang meaning for surrender.

Trace watched the flush as it worked its way up her slender neck and painted her delicate ivory skin a nice scarlet red. *I wonder if her ass will turn that same shade when she gets her first erotic spanking? I can hardly wait until I can bend her over a spanking bench and use a flogger on her. Her skin will turn every shade of pink before it goes fire engine red, then as I slide my cock deep into her tempting deep pink cunt, I'll feel the heat from her ass cheeks with each stroke.*

"Go now, Victoria, the clock is ticking." He had to suppress his chuckle as her eyes widened in surprise, and she scurried quickly from the room.

Trace's mind drifted back to his earlier thoughts about her stalker, reminding him about the message on his phone. Moving quickly to the guest bathroom across the hall, he checked the message and wasn't surprised to hear Creed's voicemail explaining he'd seen George in the area. He was, however, surprised to hear the man had been bold enough to position himself so close to ShadowDance Mountain.

Creed had assured him all the security upgrades were fully functional, and they had perimeter patrols in addition to all the electronic enhancements protecting them. Trace knew Jamie Creed well enough to hear the amusement in his voice. George thought he could outsmart everyone protecting the woman he considered his. *Oh yeah, he's fucking clueless. Alex's guys are definitely planning to play with the mouse a little before they eat it.*

Bringing himself back to the moment, he quickly texted a thank you to his friend, Mia, for all the time she'd spent with Tori, making sure she was a crack shot with a variety of small handguns as well as all Mia's romantic preparations for their return home this evening. Vowing to make sure there was a weapon nearby for Tori's easy access until this mess was resolved, he was grateful she hadn't seemed put off by the idea of firearms in their home. Just thinking about all the preparation that had taken place made the small hairs on the back of his neck stand straight up waving as if they were trying to get his attention. *Mine!*

He just couldn't keep the growl of possessiveness from rumbling from deep in his chest. No one was foolish enough to believe George was ever going to stop without being "deleted" as his Spec-Ops friends so tactfully referred to it. There wasn't a doubt in anyone's mind the man would eventually give them exactly the excuse they needed. Trace's only prayer was the chance came before the lunatic got anywhere near his wife. God but he loved the sound of that... *My wife, Tori!*

WHEN TORI REENTERED the bedroom twelve minutes later, the first thing she noticed was Trace leaning against the door of the bedroom. He had removed his shirt and boots, so he stood in his bare feet in nothing but his jeans, the top button opened, so the well-worn denim rode enticingly low on his slim hips. She let her eyes follow the light dusting of hair that trailed down his chiseled chest until it disappeared beneath his jeans. Great balls of tempting fire, the man was sex on two very long legs. She unconsciously licked her lips just thinking about where that soft trail of hair ended. When she refocused on his face, Tori knew even though his pose was casual, it was not at all relaxed.

Trace watched as Tori's eyes tracked from his impassive face down his bare chest, pausing briefly at the open top button of his jeans before continuing all the way to his bare feet. He knew many women found men's bare feet extremely erotic, but he'd never noticed a sub react so blatantly until he watched Tori's eyes all but glaze over before she pulled her gaze back up to his face. He'd managed to wait patiently, but when she licked her lips, he nearly abandoned his plan to push her a bit. Hell, all he wanted to do was toss her on the bed and lose himself inside her.

154

When he pointedly glanced at his watch, she scurried to the bed, but as she was climbing up, he spoke to her in a stern tone. "Princess, you are two minutes late." When she started to speak, he simply raised his hand to stop her.

"I gave you a deadline, and you missed it. Rules are very important in D/s relationships as is trust. Now, if I let this go, the next time I tell you to do something by a certain time or in a certain way and you don't follow my instructions, you wouldn't see any reason to comply, would you? Without consequences, instructions are meaningless. Ultimately, your trust in me will be eroded if I don't follow through, and that is unacceptable. Do you understand?"

He knew she was reeling and had suddenly found herself fighting a losing battle with apprehension. She had likely assumed it was a rhetorical question. By the time she realized he was waiting for her answer, her eyes were wide, and she only managed a quick nod. He raised an eyebrow and simply continued to wait. When she finally appeared to remember she had to use words to answer because shakes and nods of the head would not be good enough, she spoke softly.

"Yes, I understand." When he still didn't move or speak, she quickly added, "Sir."

Good girl.

He pushed off from the doorjamb and moved toward her with slow, purposeful movements. Trace loved this part of Ds sex. The anticipation of a punishment was just about the best foreplay in the whole world for both a Dom and his submissive. As he approached the bed, he caught her by the ankle and pulled her back to the edge.

Picking her up easily, he sat on the edge of the bed and laid her over his lap, so her bare ass was peaked in the perfect position for a couple of solid swats. Moving her legs apart, giving him the access he needed to trace his fingers slowly through her petal-soft folds, he was thrilled to find her soaking wet.

"Oh, my pretty baby, you are so wet for me. That makes me very happy, so I think two swats will be enough this time. That's one for each minute you were late. We'll see how well you tolerate this spanking before we make any decisions on future punishments."

All the time he'd been speaking, he'd been moving his fingers through her silky, wet folds, circling her entrance, but denying her the touch she was wiggling in a vain attempt to get.

"Oh no, my beautiful little sub, you aren't getting *that* just yet. Now, stop wiggling that gorgeous ass of yours before I have to add swats." Trace almost laughed out loud when she gasped and went instantly still. He could tell she was so turned on, he wouldn't be surprised if she came just from the spanking alone. It was a good thing she was only getting two swats.

TORI KNEW TRACE was drawing it out to enhance her anticipation, but God, waiting was about to kill her. His fingers caressing her pussy were about to drive her completely insane. *God, just a little farther forward... Argh... Please!* She didn't realize she'd spoken out loud until he laughed and simply said, "Not yet..." just before his hand landed solidly on her left ass cheek, and she heard herself cry out. *Holy shit, I wasn't ready for THAT! Fuck a duck, that hurts!*

Before she could even catch her breath, she felt him lean over her and felt his warm breath waft softly over her ear as he whispered, "Wait for it..." She didn't understand at first, but within seconds, she realized the fire in her ass cheek had sent a bolt of electricity straight to her aching clit. *Oh my God... how? Why? Ohhhhhh, that is fucking amazing!*

Just as she was beginning to process the odd connection between the pain and pleasure, Tori felt a sharp slap to the other ass cheek. This stroke hadn't shocked her as much, and she knew to ride it out. Amazingly, the blow seemed directly connected to her clit, and this time, she felt a burst of heat that felt as if every nerve ending in her body had finally been awakened.

Riding the wave of pleasure as Trace moved his fingers deep inside her, she felt her pussy gush as an unexpected orgasm raced unimpeded through her. She hadn't even known it was coming, yet it sent huge crashing waves of pleasure coursing through her entire body.

When she finally realized what had happened and felt the aftershocks begin to abate, she realized Trace had turned her over, and she was now cradled in his lap. *When did he do that?* He was holding her and whispering sweet words of praise she was finally starting to understand.

TRACE HAD BEEN stunned by her reaction to the two swats he'd given her. Hell, over the years he'd watched hundreds of subs get spankings, and he had never seen anyone as responsive as his new wife. Two moderate swats and the powerful orgasm that had obviously blindsided her had been triggered by a simple plunge of his fingers inside her gushing depths. She'd soaked his hand with her sweet cream and squeezed his fingers with such force, he'd almost been glad it hadn't been his cock. *Almost.* That thought gave him a mental chuckle. Who was he kidding, he couldn't wait until he was buried balls deep in her heat, and she squeezed him with the same force.

"You, my glorious snow angel, are in need of a new nickname. You, my love, are much too hot to be a 'snow' anything!" He smiled at her and was happy to see her shy smile. "Now, let's talk about this for a minute, and I'll remind you of the importance of complete honesty. Tell me about how you feel after your first punishment spanking."

Tori couldn't believe he wanted to have this conversation. Holy shit, was he really going to make her tell him how hot it had made her? When he remained silent, she took it as a sign he fully intended to make certain her embarrassment went all the way to her toes.

"Well, I think it's safe to say I got pretty turned on by it... but I'm confused, too." Despite her pause, Trace didn't make any effort to provide the answers he knew she was searching for. He simply waited... *the rat.*

Her mind was racing at the speed of light, trying to process all the feelings, but she wasn't having any luck sorting it all out and found herself sighing in frustration. Hopefully, he'd help her out if she made an honest attempt to draw some conclusions. She finally continued after being lost in thought for several seconds.

"I don't understand how something that was surprisingly painful on my ass could turn into white-hot need by the time it traveled the short distance to my clit. I mean, I know everything is interconnected... you know, since they are all body parts, but I really can't wrap my head around the part where the pain morphed into something else entirely. And just as you told me to wait for it, I had about a split second to wonder what you meant before the sensation racing through my clit felt like a lightning strike of pure need."

Trace was impressed with her description and astute observations. Her intelligence allowed her to process at a level far beyond what most subs would be able to see at this point. When she appeared to be finished, he responded.

"Remember, princess, the brain processes pleasure and pain in very similar ways. Also, you are obviously one of those wonderful people who has been hard-wired to react strongly to the small bite of pain that triggers your pleasure. I can't begin to tell you how thrilled I am you reacted so strongly to just a hint of real of pain. What you experienced is what people in the lifestyle refer to as erotic pain because it's so closely tied to sexual pleasure. I don't like giving out a lot of pain, it just isn't who I am. But now that I know how well you respond to a couple of swats? Well, baby, a whole new world just bloomed in 3-D Technicolor for both of us."

TORI STILL WASN'T completely clear on the connection between pain and pleasure, that much was clear from the befuddled look on her face. Trace couldn't hold back his chuckle and he softly stroked the side of her face.

"Princess, I know you don't fully comprehend the connection, but rest assured, your body understands it on a soul-deep level. All I want you to do is go along for the ride and trust me to take you where you need to go. When you let your mind shut down and allow it to merely float along and enjoy the sensations—that's when you will experience your deepest levels of pleasure and satisfaction."

Trace watched as Tori's razor-sharp mind worked to process his words. He'd learned that giving her time to work through things was the best way to help her stay in the moment. Otherwise, he had often moved onto the next thing or *two*, and she was still mulling over point one.

Laughing to himself, he sat still for a full minute until he saw she'd rejoined him. Smiling at her, he trailed the backs of his work-roughened fingers down her soft cheek. When her eyes met his again, he picked back up where he'd been in the conversation.

"You are a textbook example of why brilliant women so often find a level of freedom in submitting to their Masters they had never even imagined possible. To be able to let someone else make the decisions for even a few hours of play a week gives their souls a chance to recharge. Several subs have told me not having to worry about all the people who depend on them at work, not being held responsible for the financial futures of stockholders and being able to lose themselves in the safe, sane, and consensual atmosphere of a reputable club that caters to and thoroughly understands their kink is worth much more than their hefty membership and recurring travel expenses." At her puzzled expression, he added, "Oh, my love, we have members from all over the world. Many of them travel here several times a year, and the waiting list for the few rooms available at ShadowDance is long… very long."

"Why isn't there a motel here, then?" Tori's question was so unexpected, Trace leaned his head back and laughed out loud. He loved the way her mind worked. Hell, she'd taken his information about the club's long waiting list for their few rooms, remembered the reaction she'd gotten here at the local pub when she had asked about a motel her first night in town, and immediately worked out Climax would be able to support a small motel.

"Well, love, that is an excellent point and something I know is being discussed by the Lamonts. But while they understand the need, they don't really want to add another business to their plates right now. They are planning to spend as much time as possible with their beautiful wife and children. I believe they are considering various options but would prefer to act simply as financial backers for someone who was willing to work hard but doesn't have the start-up capital necessary to build a small motel or bed-and-breakfast." Trace watched as Tori considered his words, and God love a woman whose expressions were as good at telling a story as her words. He could see he had planted a seed, and she was working all the possibilities through in her mind.

Looking up at Trace with what he recognized as her "lawyer look," she asked, "Do you think Alex and Zach would be interested in financially backing a woman?" When he looked surprised she quickly added, "I know their lifestyle doesn't necessarily... well, sometimes it seems a bit... oh damn, I'm really going to mess this up..." Sighing, she sat back, and he could see her considering her words carefully.

Smiling to himself, Trace decided to let her off the hook.

"Tori, the men in our town are bossy and chauvinistic when it comes to the safety and pleasure of our women, but rest assured, we are all wise enough to recognize

AVERY GALE

business acumen and ability no matter the gender of the person owning it. I can assure you, Alex and Zach Lamont will be willing to listen to your idea. I'm surprised you would wonder since you have met both Jenna and Catherine."

Alex and Zach's mother, Catherine Lamont was every bit as business savvy as her husband. Daniel Lamont had always referred to his beautiful wife as his secret weapon because people were often so surprised by her beauty, they missed the brilliant business mind lurking just under the surface. And Jenna had been a wildly successful geologist and the CFO of Lamont Oil for several years before deciding to pursue a degree in counseling after marrying Colt Matthews.

"As you well know, both of those women would hold Alex and Zach's feet to the fire in a New York minute if they based a business decision on the gender of an applicant." Trace laughed to himself. *Damn but that would be mighty entertaining to watch though.* He'd known both women his entire life and had always admired their strength and grace. Watching them tag team the three Doms in their household was always entertainment at its finest.

Trace smiled when Tori responded with a deep nod of her head as if she'd just made the decision of a lifetime. When she looked directly at him and said, "I'll call them right away and—" her words were cut off when Trace grabbed her, pulling her close.

"No, my sweet subbie, we're going to go back to the subject you are so skillfully trying to avoid." While she was processing his words, he reached over the edge of the bed above head and pulled out the silk scarf he'd secured there earlier. When he manacled her wrists in his large hand and

162

moved her arms, so they were stretched over her head, he saw her eyes dilate and fill with a lust-filled apprehension.

When he'd secured her wrists, he checked to be sure they weren't so tight they would impede her circulation, then moved his hands slowly down her arms, his light touch causing her to jerk against the restraints. *So, my sweet sub is ticklish. Good to know.* He smiled at her startled look.

"Oh, princess, lawyers are champions at avoidance, I'll grant you that, but we Doms are Olympians at bringing you right back where we were when you tried to jump off the train." He laughed when she blushed a deep crimson. "See? I was right, wasn't I?

"Damn but you are a delight. I love how you keep me on my toes. I can see now the challenges and rewards with you are going to be never-ending." Standing, he quickly rolled her onto her back before securing her ankles to each of the bed posts. He stood back and watched as the blush of arousal spread over her chest, and her breathing became so quick and shallow, she was nearly panting.

Slowing his movements to heighten her anticipation, Trace rid himself of his jeans, then moved between her still-damp thighs with a catlike grace. Holding himself high enough his rock-hard cock lightly traced up and down her slit, he smiled down at her as she closed her eyes and tried to rock against him.

"I love seeing your beautiful thighs spread so far apart, my beautiful snow princess. Your pussy is so red and swollen. Knowing that is all for me is such a fucking turn on. Are you ready for your Master's possession?" Trace was thrilled with Tori's reaction to bondage, her responses nearly textbook perfect. He moved slowly, taking time to visually savor every inch of her.

"Yes, Sir," her whispered response went straight to his

cock, and he shuddered in an effort to hold back and not slam in as hard and deep as he could go.

Leaning close to her ear, Trace spoke in a softer tone, "Open your eyes, Mrs. Bartell, I want to see everything." He loved watching as Tori's eyes took on that slightly glazed-over expression as she slowly let the pleasure of his touch catch fire within her.

"You, my gorgeous wife are a vision, and I love watching as the realization I own your pleasure writes itself so clearly in your eyes, and I don't want to miss a single moment of it."

Trace heard Tori moan in pleasure as he pushed himself between her already-swollen tissues. He felt her attempts to rock back and forth, despite her restraints, and knew she was trying to get the small bit of friction it would take to push her quickly toward the release her body was chasing. He wasn't going to allow it, and when he went completely still, she cried out.

"Oh, no, no, please! Don't stop, I need to come! Oh, please."

He didn't react to Tori's desperate-sounding words because she still hadn't opened her eyes. He knew when she had finally realized her error because she opened her eyes quickly and locked onto his. He remained perfectly still as he continued to watch her intently. For long seconds, Trace didn't move or speak, he simply studied her with such an intense focus he was certain would make her uncomfortable.

"Tori, I told you I am not a heavy-handed Dom, and I dislike handing out intense levels of pain as punishments, but that does not mean I will allow you to top from the bottom... ever. Do you know what that means?"

Watching as Tori struggled to make sense of what he

had said, he knew he'd left her so on edge, she was probably having trouble just keeping up with his words, let alone being able to form any coherent thoughts of her own. She confirmed his suspicions when she finally managed to squeak out.

"I… um… oh God, Trace I can't answer questions now! You're scrambling my brain. *Argh!*" Trace had leaned back, so her pearly pink clit was nice and exposed, and his light slap directly atop the delicate tissues had her gasping for breath.

"Watch your tone, sweetness. I can keep you dancing right on the edge of release for hours if I want to, so I suggest you make a real diligent effort to answer my question." Trace loved how responsive Tori was to his domination, and he was sure it wouldn't be long until regular vanilla sex didn't hold any appeal for her at all which would be fine as far as he was concerned. He could see she was struggling to focus enough to remember what he'd asked her. Deciding to help her just a bit, he repeated the question.

"Princess, I asked you if you know what 'topping from the bottom' means."

"Oh frack… um… No, I don't know for sure… oh God, please…" Tori's voice was becoming increasingly ragged, her breathing little more than shallow panting, and he knew she was finding herself awash in the sensations as he used an ever-so-slight rotation of his hips, so the blunt end of his rock-hard cock brushed up against her sweet spot, while at the same time he drew circles around her throbbing clit, never hitting the top, knowing that small touch was all it would take to send her over instantly. Christ, she was just so fucking perfect for him, it was beyond humbling. He loved how his brilliant wife was rendered nearly speechless under his hand.

"Ohhhh, please! Um… I think it must be trying to be the boss when I'm not supposed to be. Is that it? Or at least close? Damn it all, can you at least give me a hint? Please, can I come now? Is the quiz over?"

Trace had to bite the insides of his mouth to suppress his smile. Damn, she was so adorable. Sassy, but adorable. A quick pinch to her nipples brought her up almost off the bed.

"Watch your sass, princess. Remember who is in charge when we are in this room or the playroom or the club. Hell, let's just make it a clean slate, shall we?" With that, he began thrusting into her rippling channel with long, deep strokes before he finished. "Let's just leave it that it is my right, duty, and honor to be in charge of your safety, happiness, orgasms, and most everything else you can imagine. Now. Come now!"

Tori's response was immediate, and Trace was sure her body had hurtled itself over the edge of bliss before her mind even had the chance to register the command. He used his hands to hold her down as much for her safety as to give her the feeling of total restraint he knew she loved. *Damn, babe, I'm afraid you are going to bruise your wrists and ankles. Hell, if you hadn't been tied down, you would have thrashed yourself right off this bed.*

It only took Trace a few more strokes to find his own release. His pleasure had been accelerated by the strength of her orgasm. Stilling inside her, he gave himself a few seconds to catch his breath and enjoy the rippling after-shocks caressing his cock. When he finally caught his breath, he looked into her eyes and relished the sated expression he saw moving over her beautiful face. Reaching over her head, he untied her wrists and smiled at her groan when he shifted just enough to pull the silk ties from her ankles as well. As his cock shifted within her, he felt her muscles ripple around him as after-shocks continued to move through her pelvis.

"I'm going to roll to the side and stay inside you as we drift off to sleep for a couple of reasons, princess. First, I want to keep my seed inside your body for as long as possible, the caveman in me wants to beat my chest in triumph knowing I've planted it so deep in your womb. I also want you to feel the full depth of my love for you, my ownership of your body just a small part of that love, but it's a part I want you to be thinking about as we fall to sleep in each other's arms."

Rolling gently to his side and tucking her head under his chin, so he could feel each soft breath she took, he smiled and took great satisfaction when she snuggled as close as possible to him and let herself slide almost instantly into a deep sleep.

He'd been pleased when she had mentioned recently since she'd been sleeping wrapped in his arms, she hadn't had a recurrence of the nightmares that had plagued her for the past year. He was thrilled to see the dark shadows, so prominent under her beautiful eyes when he'd first met her, had slowly faded away—another testament to the fact she was finally able to get the rest she needed so badly. On the rare occasions she'd become restless in her sleep, she always settled immediately when he'd pulled her close and whispered reassurances she was safe in her ear. Knowing she responded to him even in sleep was deeply satisfying.

Chapter 16

T RACE HAD RELUCTANTLY agreed to leave Tori at home alone only because he was confident she was being protected by a state-of-the-art security system that had been fully activated as soon as they returned home from their honeymoon. After the FBI agents alerted local authorities that Tori's stalker had gone off grid in Texas, Colt and Dylan had put together a crack team of security professionals of their own because frankly, they had seen the Feds blow enough cases to be convinced taking additional precautions was time and money well invested.

With the temperatures on ShadowDance Mountain hovering just below freezing, no one had expected George to make a water entry, so they were several seconds behind him when he silently cut through the glass doors on the deck surrounding the second story of the Bartell ranch home. When Creed speed dialed Tori, her phone went straight to voicemail. He didn't waste time leaving a message, this would all be over in the time it took her to even retrieve it. Cursing, he dialed Trace.

"We have a breach of second-floor deck—my ETA is three minutes—where are you?" Creed's tone was quick, and his words were military brief.

"Fuck! How? Goddamn it, I'm just leaving the feed store in town. I'm at least ten out." Trace couldn't believe he'd left Tori alone. He'd tried to get her to ride along, but she'd pleaded for a bit of "girl time," reminding him "beauty doesn't just happen" and saying she needed some time to attend to "details" if he expected her to be ready to attend dinner at the Lamonts', then go to the club later this evening.

Jamie knew Trace had been lost in the guilt of leaving her, and even though he understood it, he needed Trace back in the game. "Bartell, focus—what was Tori planning to do and where was her weapon?"

"Her gun was beside the bed, and she wanted some girl time, so I'm assuming she is taking a nice leisurely bath." Jamie heard Trace cursing as he tried to manage the phone and rational thought all the while driving at a breakneck pace. Trace finally continued, "Fuck, I hope she took her weapon and phone with her. Did you try to call her? Hell, maybe we shouldn't scare her. How did he get past everyone? Goddamn it!"

Creed could hear the sounds of squealing tires and horns and knew Trace would be driving like a NASCAR champion. Having him hurt or hurting someone else wasn't going to help anybody.

"Hey, man, I know you're worried about her, but you can't possibly get here before this goes down. Killing yourself or someone else won't help Tori—Be Safe—Out."

Heeding Creed's warning, Trace tried to slow down. He remembered exactly what it felt like to lose someone to the negligence of another person who was behind the wheel when they shouldn't be. He and the young man who'd killed his wife would always live with the consequences of his poor decision that night. Trace knew they were both slowly rebuilding their lives, and that was as it should be. But now, the life he'd been so sure was finally back on track was once again on the verge of going terribly wrong. Not wanting to be responsible for bringing the kind of pain and desolation he'd experienced into anyone else's life and particularly, not his new bride's, Trace slowed his pace and refocused his attention of the task at hand— getting to Tori—safely. *Creed's going to get her, and she's going to need me, and I'll be there for her... today and always!*

TORI KNEW TRACE would be proud of her for remembering to bring her small pistol into the bath with her. She'd moved her bath sheet to cover it after placing the small-caliber weapon next to the miniature pool Trace called a bathtub. One of the main purposes of a lavender-scented bubble bath was to relax, and she'd been distracted by the gleaming metal of a deadly weapon laying out in plain sight. It wasn't distracting her as long as it wasn't out in plain view. *Oh, husband mine, you will be so proud of me.*

Just as she lowered herself into a lavender-scented water version of heaven, she thought about her cell phone. *Damn... I have kept that phone within reach for months. Hell, it's been nearly an obsession for over a year. What was I thinking not grabbing that, too?* Then blowing out a frustrated sigh, she remembered she'd let the battery go dead because her charger was still in Trace's truck. She made a mental note to get it and her laptop from the backseat as soon as he returned. They had both been so tired when they had finally returned home last night, they hadn't bothered to bring in anything but the barest of necessities.

Even though they'd been nearly dead on their feet, she couldn't help smiling as she recalled the brief stop they'd made at the Lamonts.' Laying back and just letting the warm water work its magic on her aching muscles, Tori let her mind wander back to the joy she'd felt when they'd entered the bedroom last night. She'd been so touched by his friends' efforts to make their first night back home extra special. *It takes an extraordinary man to inspire that level of loyalty from his friends.*

Tori was continually amazed by how much her life had changed in such a short amount of time. She'd left behind a job she'd loved in the beginning, but as the stalking had gotten worse, her coworkers and friends had pulled back one by one, all except Layla.

Smiling to herself, she thought about the tall, blonde bombshell receptionist who worked for the law firm where Tori had worked. Layla Lange had proved to be the bravest person she'd ever met. Tori hadn't been joking when she'd told Trace her sweet friend hadn't hesitated to stand up for her.

Layla had blatantly lied to Gary George on several occasions, and on others, she had sent him on wild goose chases or distracted him to allow Tori enough time to slip out one of the side doors.

Everyone else had been worried about being caught in the crossfire and becoming collateral damage, but Layla had only worried about doing what was right. She'd waved Tori off several times when she'd tried to thank her friend for her efforts, insisting no one should be thanked for "just doing the right thing."

Laughing to herself, Tori remembered meeting Layla after work one night for drinks after the Blonde Tornado had blown "Stalkerman," as Layla had dubbed him, right back out the front doors of the office building where they worked. Layla had grabbed the bouquet of flowers out of his hand and swatted him with them all the way out the front, leaving a trail of floral destruction in her path. When Tori had come down the hall just in time to see Gary stalking off down the sidewalk, she'd taken in the flower stems and petals littering the floor and burst out laughing.

Unfortunately, her laughter had soon been followed by racking sobs. Layla had gotten them both out of the building quickly, and a few minutes later, they'd been sipping the most enormous margaritas Tori had ever seen. They'd talked late into the night about everything and nothing.

God, I wish I had Layla nearby to talk to. Kat, Jenna, and Rissa would so love her... damn, but we'd all have fun together!

Because of her appearance, Layla was continually underestimated. The woman was a modern-day version of Marilyn Monroe except for her Mensa-worthy IQ. Tori knew about all the hours her friend spent studying, and she was filled with pride knowing Layla would be graduating Summa Cum Laude from The University of Texas in Houston with a Master of Science degree in Business this coming May.

The woman was fierce in everything she did despite a very rocky personal history. Tori made a mental note to ask Mitch Grayson if there was a way she could securely e-mail Layla and invite her to visit after her graduation. Sighing softly, she tried to relax back in the warm water and consider all the ways her life had been affected by the relentless stalking of a man she'd only gone to dinner with once. But focusing on all the horrible things he'd done wasn't going to accomplish anything, so she tried to refocus her thinking. She needed to remember that without fate playing out the way it had, she would have never considered coming to Colorado when she'd received the letter about her surprise windfall. She would have never met Trace, and even though they hadn't been together very long, her had soul recognized him as a good man from the moment she'd looked up into his eyes as she sat in the snow in front of that crazy bar. No, she wasn't going to focus on what she'd lost, rather she would look at what she'd gained, and she couldn't imagine her life without Trace in it.

GARY GEORGE COULD smell lavender as he made his way through the enormous bedroom. Pausing beside the bed, he thought the top of his head was going to blow clear off as he envisioned Victoria giving herself to the fucking cowboy she'd sold herself to. Christ, didn't the woman have any taste at all? Knowing she had been willing to share with this two-bit mountain man what she'd denied him was infuriating. Deciding he'd need to add another "punishment" for that sent a surge of blood to his groin, but really, what did it matter? He was going to torture and kill her, anyway.

Keeping score seemed like a waste of effort when you looked at the bigger picture. He knew he was doing society a huge favor by taking women like Victoria Paulson off the streets. *Yeah, dick teases—all of them. The world is better off without them. Leaves righteous women like his sweet mama with more options, yes, that's what it does. Hell, I ought to get a fucking Nobel Prize or something.*

Putting his thoughts of her having sex in this bed aside, he moved toward the partially closed bathroom door. Standing to the side, he focused on her reflection in the mirror. She really was a beautiful woman, but his admiration wasn't enough to earn her a reprieve from her fate. Several of the women he'd killed had been stunning, but their beauty was lost forever as soon as he took a knife to them. Their blood and screams and the stench of coming death had filled his senses. For a few seconds, he was lost in the memory of how turned on he became each time he watched one of them take their last breath.

Shaking himself out of his musings, he stood watching Tori for a few seconds, thinking about how satisfying it was going to feel watching his knife slice through her ivory skin. Fucking the women he'd killed had never been his driving force, it had always just a very pleasant side benefit. Feeling his body start to respond with arousal at the sight of Victoria lying back, wet and naked, he shifted his stance to relieve the pressure of his dick, trying to press itself through the zipper of his pants. As he moved to adjust his rapidly responding cock, his elbow bumped the wall, and even though the sound was barely audible, he froze in place. He barely breathed as he watched her face for any sign she'd heard him.

DESPITE THE FACT Tori had been drifting in a sort of relaxed fog, the small thump just outside the door brought her back instantly. She barely managed to keep her eyes closed, and instinctively, she knew staying calm and not letting an intruder know she was aware of their presence was her only advantage, well, at least until she could get her hand on the small pistol lying under her towel.

Running through the facts had always been Tori's way

of dealing with stressful situations, and this was no exception. First, she knew the alarms would have been triggered by his entrance into the house. She briefly wondered how he had gotten close enough when there were perimeter systems out there that rivaled top-secret military installations, but she quickly dismissed those thoughts as not useful at this point. Planning exactly how she was going to pretend to come awake slowly, then gracefully stand, so the water would sluice seductively down her body was useful. *Hey, a distraction is a distraction, and right now I don't have many options to work with, so I'm going to use anything and everything at my disposal.*

She'd reach down and palmed the small gun in her right hand when she picked up the bath sheet. She wasn't sure how she was going to conceal the fact she was holding a gun while drying herself, but she'd just have to wing that part.

Gary George was relieved Victoria hadn't heard the small sound his elbow had made when he'd bumped against the wall. Christ, that had been a heart-stopping moment as he had held his breath, watching for any sign the sleeping slut had heard him. When he saw her start to stretch and move, he decided to just let her give him a little peep show. Hell, she'd be easier to handle if she wasn't all slick and wet, anyway. He almost laughed out loud at his own play on words.

Bitch, you are going to be slick and wet for me soon enough. As soon as I find a nice secluded spot out in those woods, we'll be revisiting slick and wet, yes indeed.

CREED FINALLY MADE his way to the house and was slowly moving up the stairs when he heard the distinctive sound of someone moving around in water. Rolling his eyes, he silently sent up a prayer that Tori would be covered by the time the prick who'd made his way into her home found his way to her. The thought of her being exposed to her stalker while naked nearly made him hurl. Just as he hit the upstairs hallway, he heard a small gasp a split second before the sound of Tori screaming filled the air.

TORI KEPT THE gun hidden in the palm of her hand and was almost dry when she looked up in the mirror and locked eyes with Gary George. Even though she'd known it had to be him, she was still so startled, she gasped and screamed.

"What are you doing here? You can't be here! Get out!" She knew she was wasting her breath, but every second they spent talking was another second closer the cavalry would be, and she knew they had to be making their way to her.

"Think you're pretty fucking smart taking off, don't you, bitch? I told you that you were mine and only mine. You'll never belong to the hick cowboy you've been fucking." His voice sent shivers up Tori's spine, it sounded like something Hollywood would come up with for a demon. When he realized she wasn't reacting, he barked, "Get your hot little body dried, but don't use that towel between your legs. I want you to have to feel that wetness turn to ice as you walk out of this place for the last time."

"What do you mean the last time? I'm not going any-where with you. I know you're being watched. You've killed other women, haven't you?" Tori knew she was poking the bear, but she had to keep him talking, so she could get in position to shoot. Right now, he was standing far enough around the corner she didn't have a clear shot, and she was certain she was going to get one... and only one chance.

CREED COULDN'T BELIEVE what he was hearing. *Holy fuck, woman, don't antagonize his psycho ass!* Before he could enter the room, he heard Tori speaking again and decided to hit his mic with the signal for Grayson to record. As he listened, it occurred to him she was not only stalling for time, she intended to get a confession that would put the bastard behind bars for the rest of his life. Knowing he could only let it go on for a minute or two at the max before the house was swarming with his team, he decided to give the lady her chance. He could see George in the reflection of the mirror hanging above the headboard of the Trace and Tori's massive bed. The prick didn't have a gun trained on her, and Creed knew he would be able to take the bastard out before he ever drew his piece.

GARY LEANED AGAINST the doorjamb as if this conversation was an everyday occurrence and let his eyes move over every inch of her exposed flesh before he answered.

"You think you've got it all figured out, huh?" He paused for several long heartbeats before his eyes returned to hers, and she shivered at their cold depths.

She didn't think she'd ever seen eyes that were nothing but pools of absolute emptiness, and Tori swore to herself she would remember that look as long as she lived... which wouldn't be long if he got his hands on her.

"You are the only woman I ever considered keeping. If you had just returned my feelings, you wouldn't have had to go to all this trouble, and I wouldn't be here looking at your lush naked body, thinking about how great it's going to feel to finally fuck you. Maybe I should just hang out and let lover boy watch, huh? Think he'd enjoy watching while I ream every hole you've got before I start slicing and dicing his new wife?"

Tori was shifting ever so slowly, so she would finally be facing the pure evil that was Gary George. Pretending to stumble back in her nervousness, she used the cover of that move to mask the small snick as she released the safety on the pistol she still hadn't revealed.

"I don't understand. Why me? You're a good-looking guy, you shouldn't have any trouble attracting women." Tori was enraged but had managed to keep her voice shaky, so he'd believe she was nearly mindless with fear. He seemed to be the most relaxed and comfortable when he had the upper hand, and she wasn't ready to play her ace, just yet.

"Oh, I never had any trouble getting any of the whores I killed to leave a bar or restaurant with me. You know you are the only one out of a dozen I even bought a meal? Christ, you were one expensive date and don't think I didn't know the minute you discounted me. Just before you ordered dessert, you decided I was just another punch meal ticket, didn't you?"

Tori was actually surprised he had been that tuned in

during their date since he hadn't managed to stop talking about himself for more than thirty seconds during their entire evening together. She wasn't about to admit he'd hit it so close to dead center, not just yet, anyway.

"That isn't true, I really hadn't thought about it until you took me home. You were just so forceful and sure of yourself. Well, you kind of overwhelmed me." Deciding she needed to direct the conversation rather than just answering him, she quickly added, "Have you really killed a dozen women? How did you get away with it? You must be extremely intelligent to have eluded capture for so long." Trying to interject a small amount of admiration into her voice almost made her skin crawl, but she only needed to stall for one more subtle shift in her position, then she'd be ready.

He pushed himself from the door and took a step toward her before he spoke. "I am the police, you dimwitted cunt. Do you really think I wouldn't know exactly how to direct and distract the investigation? Jesus, some of those detectives are as dumb as a box of rocks, I tell you. Stupid fuckers wouldn't let me transfer to homicide because I didn't have a fucking college degree, so I wasn't as smart as them. Well, who's the smart one now?"

Tori swore she saw his eyes practically glow as the evil inside him continued to spew forth. Just as she was ready to speak again, he raised his hand to reveal a wicked looking knife, the blade at least seven inches long and reflected the light in ways that told her it had been sharpened to the point, it would slide through flesh and muscle with equal ease. His feral smile let her know the time for talking was over even before he practically shouted at her.

"Move on out of there, let's get going. I'm done answering all your ignorant, fucking questions."

Tori watched his eyes widen as he took in the sight of the gun she had pulled from the towel while his eyes had been locked on hers. "Don't move, or I *will* shoot you." Tori could tell by the way his eyes flashed and his lips twitched, he didn't believe her for a second. She watched his eyes just as Mia had taught her to. *Wait for it... wait for it.* Oh yeah, there it was, the small blink just before he lunged, and her reaction was instantaneous.

Pulling the trigger was the easiest decision she'd ever made. There was not one single part of her that was going to allow him to hurt her or any other woman ever again. Watching as red bloomed across his chest and his expression went from anger to shock, she pulled the trigger again, placing the second shot right between his eyes.

As he fell face first at her feet, the knife he'd been clutching skittered across the floor just as Jamie Creed burst into the room with his gun drawn. Looking down at the very dead man on the floor, Creed used the toe of his boot to flip him over and smiled.

"Goddamn, Tori, nice shooting. Holy hell, if you weren't already married, I'd propose on the spot." Tori looked up at him with wide eyes, and he realized that she was rapidly skating toward a meltdown. Jamie crossed the distance between them in a split second, realizing she was a breath away from adrenaline crash.

"Oh, shit. Hey, it's okay. You did great. You are kick ass you know that?" He quickly holstered his gun and wrapped her in the robe he found on the counter. When he had her covered, he scooped her up and moved quickly down the hall. Just as he reached the top of the stairs, Trace barreled through the front door.

Creed thought for just a second the giant of a man standing in front of him might sag to the floor when he saw him holding Tori. Jamie watched as relief flooded Trace's expression at the sight of his sweet and uninjured wife, but he recovered quickly as Jamie handed her off.

"Hey, man, glad you're here. I'll stay here by the door and wait for Dylan and crew. By my calculations, they are about a minute out. Take Tori into the living room and get her settled. Watch for shock, but damn, I gotta tell you, that is one hell of a woman you're holding. She did you proud, man."

Creed opened the front door to wait for the surge of people who were quickly making their way up the front walk as Trace moved to the living room with Tori cradled in his arms.

JUST AS TRACE had stepped from his truck, he heard two gunshots and had nearly lost his mind in the few seconds it had taken him to race into the house. When he'd opened the door and saw Creed carrying Tori down the stairs, he had finally been able to take a breath. It had taken everything in him to not to drop to his knees in sheer relief. While he'd held her in their living room, he thought back and realized he didn't even remember walking the short distance before collapsing on to the soft leather sofa facing the warm fire flickering in the fireplace. Just as she had started to shake, Zach appeared at his side. He sat the medic bag by Trace's feet and began checking her pulse and respiration.

Zach asked for her permission to give her a small sedative, and at her silent nod, the former medic made short work of giving her the injection, all the while praising her for her quick thinking and her calm during the crisis. Zach softly explained that Creed had activated his mic and their entire conversation had been recorded. He smiled at Tori and congratulated her on her fine shooting skills.

Tori hadn't spoken a word since the shooting, had barely reacted to anything happening around her, until Zach said, "You know, Tori, Alex and I have been thinking that Kat needs to learn to shoot, maybe you and Mia could teach a class?"

Zach's grin told her he was only half kidding, and for some reason, that seemed to snap her back to herself, and she looked up at him and smiled before answering, "I think that can be arranged." As soon as she'd re-engaged, Trace caught Zach's subtle nod as he moved on, evidently satisfied the beautiful woman resting in her husband's lap was going to be fine.

Trace wasn't sure he was going to recover as quickly though. Damn, he felt like all of his blood had been drained from his body. Watching Zach move to the long bar along the wall, Zach poured himself and Trace a glass of his expensive Scotch. When he handed one of the heavy crystal glasses to Trace, he had raised his with a nod toward Tori.

"Here's to our warrior wives, damn but I'm proud of them."

Trace heard the words and realized he hadn't said a single word to the bravest woman he'd ever known to let her know just how much he admired her. He quickly downed the Scotch, letting it scorch its way all the way down his parched throat before setting the heavy tumbler aside and nodding to Zach in silent thanks for his efforts to pull him back from the edge.

Zach smiled and patted his knee before standing and

making an excuse about needing to get back to Shadow-Dance before Kat had to deal with three screaming babies all alone. Trace's heart warmed each time he thought about the Lamont triplets. It wasn't often in this age of technology that a baby was able to avoid detection, but that is exactly what little Mary Catherine had done. She'd hidden behind her two brothers until her birthday, surprising everybody with her sudden appearance. Trace realized Tori was looking at him, her eyes questioning his goofy grin, so he did the only thing he could do, he kissed her.

Chapter 17

TORI REMEMBERED THINKING she must have fallen into some kind of gelatin because her movements seemed lethargic and everything was just a little fuzzy around the edges as Jamie Creed had carried her down the hall and made his way down the staircase without so much as jiggling her, and why she had even noticed *that* was another puzzle piece.

Nothing had seemed to be making any sense until she'd seen Trace standing in the doorway. Her heart had nearly stopped when she saw him, and if she hadn't been floundering around in that blasted gelatin, she'd have leaped out of Jamie Creed's arms and into the loving arms of her new husband. Just his touch, his unique outdoorsy scent, and the feel of his cheek pressing against the top of her head was enough to pull her back closer to reality.

He had settled her on his lap and kept touching her as if checking and rechecking to assure himself she was indeed unharmed. Once her brain re-engaged, Tori had started to shake, and it seemed like the tremors were radiating from her very core to quake their way to the surface. She heard Zach Lamont ask her permission to give her something to calm her and help her center herself, and she had only been able to nod her acquiescence. Whatever he'd given her had worked almost immediately, and while it had calmed her, it hadn't made her groggy, and she was grateful for that.

Tori finally pulled herself back from Trace after a kiss that was nothing but pure relief. She put just enough distance between them to be able to look into his eyes. The love she saw reflected in his expression made her eyes flood with tears.

"It's over. It's really over. Oh, Trace, he was such a horrible man. He killed so many women, and he was going to kill me, too. And he wanted to rape me while he made you watch. But I shot him. I did just what Mia taught me. I didn't hesitate. I just got in position, waited for the blink, and pulled the trigger. Maybe it makes me a bad person, but I don't even feel bad about taking his life. He was so evil. Oh, God, I'm babbling... I know it, and I can't help myself... oh damn, now I know how Kat feels..." Feeling the tears running in steady streams down her cheeks, she brushed them away with the backs of her hands and took a deep breath, trying to regain some semblance of control over her runaway mouth.

When Trace didn't say anything but sat quietly studying her, she started to panic. Finally, she couldn't stand the silence any longer, and she looked up at him again from under lashes that were heavy with her tears.

"Do you still want me? I mean, I'll understand if you don't want to be married to someone who killed another person." Taking a deep breath and letting it out, she looked at her hands clasped in her lap, too afraid to look at him, terrified she'd just blown her chances at the life she had always dreamed of.

TRACE HAD BEEN so totaled by the adrenaline crash, it was a few seconds before Tori's question fully registered in his mind... *What the fuck? Is she serious? What the hell?* He finally got himself together enough to answer.

"Oh, Tori, my love, of course, I want you... I am in awe of you. I'm sorry if you misunderstood my silence. Hell, I was so far beyond terrified when Creed called and said someone had broken into the house... and I had to drive all the way home... I have never felt so helpless in my entire life. Every time I blinked, I saw you having to face your worst nightmare, and I felt swamped by guilt for not being here when you needed me the most."

Trace felt as if the floodgates of his emotions had finally opened, and he just needed to let it all out, so the amazing woman in his arms understood exactly how much she meant to him.

"When I opened the door and saw Creed holding you safely in his arms, I was so thankful, it took everything I had to keep from falling to my knees in relief. And when I finally had you in my arms, all I could think of was how humbled I am to have been given another second chance." He pulled her tight against his chest and rubbed her back with slow, soothing circles as she sobbed.

Tori didn't know if she was crying with relief Trace still wanted her or because everything that had happened was finally catching up with her, but the great gulping sobs seemed like they would never end. When she was finally totally spent, she sagged against his completely soaked shirt, hiccupping as the last bits of emotion finally drained away.

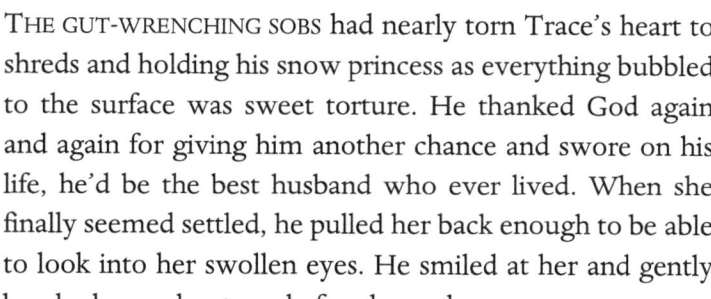

THE GUT-WRENCHING SOBS had nearly torn Trace's heart to shreds and holding his snow princess as everything bubbled to the surface was sweet torture. He thanked God again and again for giving him another chance and swore on his life, he'd be the best husband who ever lived. When she finally seemed settled, he pulled her back enough to be able to look into her swollen eyes. He smiled at her and gently brushed away her tears before he spoke.

"Tori, you are the greatest gift I've ever received. I'll spend the rest of my life showing you just how much I love you and how grateful I am you are my wife. I can't begin to tell you how proud I am of how you handled yourself today. You are my life, every breath I take is for you."

Tori listened to Trace's sweet words, and her heart melted. He'd just repeated his marriage vows to her, proving nothing had changed in a way he knew would go straight to her heart and soul. She wrapped her arms around his neck, buried her face in the warmth of his neck, and repeated her vows to him.

"I love you. You are the answer to every prayer I've ever whispered about the perfect husband. I don't know what I did to deserve you... but I'm glad somebody up there was watching when it happened."

BOOKS BY AVERY GALE

The ShadowDance Club
Katarina's Return – Book One
Jenna's Submission – Book Two
Rissa's Recovery – Book Three
Trace & Tori – Book Four
Reborn as Bree – Book Five
Red Clouds Dancing – Book Six
Perfect Picture – Book Seven

Club Isola
Capturing Callie – Book One
Healing Holly – Book Two
Claiming Abby – Book Three

Masters of the Prairie Winds Club
Out of the Storm
Saving Grace
Jen's Journey
Bound Treasure
Punishing for Pleasure
Accidental Trifecta
Missionary Position
Another Second Chance
Star-Crossed Miracles
Dusted Star
Lilly's Choice

The Wolf Pack Series
Mated – Book One
Fated Magic – Book Two
Tempted by Darkness – Book Three

The Knights of the Boardroom
Book One
Book Two
Book Three

The Morgan Brothers of Montana
Coral Hearts – Book One
Dancing with Deception – Book Two
Caged Songbird – Book Three
Game On – Book Four
Well Bred – Book Five

Mountain Mastery
Well Written
Savannah's Sentinel
Sheltering Reagan

Enchanted Holidays
The Christmas Painting

I would love to hear from you!

Website:
www.averygale.com

Facebook:
facebook.com/avery.gale.3

Twitter:
@avery_gale